THE GATEKEEPERS OF DEMOCRACY

THE GATEKEEPERS OF DEMOCRACY

BILL LEWERS

CONTENTS

DEDICATION

On "the first Tuesday after the first Monday" in November untold thousands of women and men volunteer to serve as election officers. Putting their day-to-day lives and political persuasions on hold, they gather in school gymnasiums and cafeterias; in parish halls and town libraries; in community centers and senior citizen residences. There, for fifteen hours or more, they expend their time, energy, skill, and integrity so that we may freely and fairly choose our leaders. It is to these, "the gatekeepers of democracy," that this book is dedicated.

Author's Notes and Acknowledgements

*T*HE GATEKEEPERS OF *Democracy* is a work of fiction. Its people, places, and events exist only in my imagination. Nonetheless the inspiration for writing the story has come from the twenty plus years of service that I have been privileged to give to the electoral process in Fairfax County, Virginia, first as an election officer, then a chief election officer, and most recently as a "rover." During this time I have served with and under some marvelous individuals who have touched me with their talent, dedication, and kindness. The example set by these "gatekeepers of democracy" has made this story possible.

While the narrative is fiction, its environment comes primarily from the election code of the state of Virginia and the electoral practices of Fairfax County. Even here however, I have felt free to modify these codes and practices for the sake of telling a story. Hence while I do believe the book gives a realistic feel of what it is like to serve as an election officer, a number of the details will not match the current code and practices of any specific state or locality. Ultimately this a story written to entertain, not an election manual.

I would like to thank my three beta readers: Catherine Mathews of the Great Falls Writer's Group, Mary Marlow Lewers, and Barbara Lewers. Each of them provided many useful suggestions for improving the narrative as well as uncovering many typos. I am very much in their debt. One of their suggestions was to provide a glossary of election related terms which I have included at the end of the book.

In addition the members of the Great Falls Writers Group and especially its founder and facilitator Kristin Clark Taylor, have been a source of support and encouragement in my writing over the past two years.

Any set of acknowledgements must conclude with my sons, Mark and John, and my wife Mary who fill my life with joy and meaning each and every day.

1

TUESDAY, JANUARY 6, 5:30 P.M.

THE PAIN WAS excruciating.

Her head throbbed. Her left cheekbone felt like it had been ripped raw. In fact the entire left side of her face felt battered and bruised. Pain shot up and down her left arm at regular intervals. And her wrist drilled her with a relentless dull ache.

She reached over with her right hand and with a single finger touched her left wrist. The dull ache instantly became searing pain. For a moment she was afraid she might pass out but a couple of deep breaths put her back in control. She then tried wiggling the fingers of her hand. They responded, somewhat. Next she extended the hand so as to touch the wall of the store. More pain.

At least nothing's numb, she thought. *I guess that's good.*

Holding the folder in her right hand, close to her body, she looked out into the parking lot. What had started as a cold drizzle had gradually become steadier. More and more portions of the parking lot appeared to have frozen over. She looked down at her low heeled shoes; soaked, caked with mud, and probably ruined. Why hadn't she changed to the boots? So stupid.

Well, I'm not getting it done just standing here, she reflected. Her two seater sports car was in the first row of the parking lot but she still had to navigate the icy pavement in her compromised condition. Ever so slowly she inched forward testing the pavement for firmness before committing herself. Her feet were soaked to the bone and so very cold. Gradually she worked her way toward the car, taking small, measured steps. At last she reached it. Even a simple thing like unlocking the door was torment as she transferred the folder ever so gently to her left arm and used her right hand to locate the car key. A single click, and the car door was unlocked.

It was not until she got into the driver's seat, placing the folder on the seat next to her that she realized that ice had formed on the windshield.

"Oh damn," she said struggling to get out of the car.

Once outside she realized that she did not have the ice scrapper with her. Not wanting to do another round trip to retrieve it, she pried the ice from the wipers with her fingers and then ran her entire right arm back and forth across the windshield. Satisfied that it was more or less clear, she got back into the car.

She started the car and turned on the headlights. Looking ahead she studied the ramp leading out of the parking lot onto the road. It looked icy to her; how icy she could not say. She managed to secure her seat belt and then tried gripping the steering wheel with her left hand. Her fingers did manage to wrap around the wheel, albeit painfully. Good. At least she would not have to drive the car with one hand.

Well I guess I'll just have to gun it up the ramp and hope for the best, she thought.

She stepped tentatively on the accelerator. The wheels spun at first but after a couple of seconds found traction. She approached the ramp and stepped harder on the gas. Up the ramp the car went. She could feel the car's tires battling with the icy pavement.

At one point the rear wheels spun out to the right but she pressed even harder on the accelerator and the car miraculously righted itself. At last the car reached the top of the ramp.

Looking out onto the road, she was glad to see that the moving cars had thus far prevented any freezing on the pavement. She put on the left turn signal and made the entry into traffic without incident.

Once in traffic she began to think past her immediate pain and wondered how she would be received when she reached her destination. They had all expected her to return sooner. So had she. *Would they be upset that it had taken so long? Would he be upset that it had taken her so long?*

At last it came into view. She signaled another left turn and navigated the car into the parking lot. The building was to the right, but she turned her car in the opposite direction and pulled into a far row where four other cars were parked.

Having safely parked the car, she took a moment to gather herself together. The acuteness of her pain reasserted itself and she suddenly felt tired; desperately tired. She looked up at herself in the rear view mirror and shuddered. What a mess.

Slowly she got out of the car, holding onto the precious folder. Her body ached and her destination looked so far away. She started to walk toward the building. The cold pellets of rain beat down on her, stinging her face, and penetrating her already soaked clothing. The closer she got, the harder it was. At last she reached the sidewalk. The near door was closed shut while the one farther away was ajar, illuminated by a bright, welcoming light.

She reached the near door and tried pushing it open. It would not budge. She then tried turning the handle. Nothing. At last she started pounding on the door with her good right hand.

"Let me in," she cried. "For God's sake, let me in!"

2

TUESDAY, NOVEMBER 4, THE PREVIOUS YEAR

CARL MARSDEN WAS standing near the corner of the gymnasium at the Chesterbrook Elementary School when he saw the lady enter at about 1:30 in the afternoon. With her gray hair and weathered face, he would have taken her to be about seventy-five years of age. She looked around the gym and then hesitantly approached the voter check-in table where the election officers were enjoying their first bit of "down time" after a very busy morning. She conversed with them for a moment and then one of the officers signaled for Carl to join them.

"My father would like to vote," she said adding almost apologetically,

"He is in the car. I don't think he will be able to come inside."

Carl smiled reassuringly.

"Not a problem, ma'am. May I see his ID?"

The woman produced the needed ID. Carl led her over to the check-in table where the electronic pollbooks were.

"Can you look this up, Nancy?" he said to the African American woman behind the table. Nancy Jordan was the Chesterbook precinct's assistant chief election officer. She and Carl had worked together for a number of years. They were of different political parties as all chief-assistant chief duos were required to be but they worked well together. He liked Nancy but more important he respected her commitment to making the political process work. She quickly keyed in the man's name and it appeared on the computer screen. Carl saw that he was well into his nineties.

"Matthew Borden, 1200 Montgomery Avenue," spoke Nancy in a clear voice.

One of the poll watchers at the table directly behind wrote the name down on her pad.

"Don't confirm him in the pollbook until I do a visual with the photo," he whispered to Nancy. She nodded, indicating her understanding.

Having observed this legality, Carl took a "ballot card" from the check-in table and led Matthew Borden's daughter over to the ballot table to obtain his ballot. He presented the ballot card to the officer at the table and secured the ballot enclosed in a privacy folder for Mr. Borden.

The ballot card generally served as a ticket to let the officer at the ballot table know that the voter had been checked in and was entitled to vote. It was an essential part of the process when the precinct was busy. Carl knew that with the gym temporarily devoid of other voters, many chiefs would not have bothered with this formality. He, however, believed in doing everything "by the book." There had been some resistance to his strict (some said "slavish") adherence to every little rule and technicality when he joined this team as chief election officer some five years earlier but these issues had long since been resolved.

Putting together the ballot, privacy folder, clipboard, pen, and (just in case) a *Request for Assistance* form, Carl asked to be led to Mr. Borden's car.

As he neared the car, he observed the silhouette of an individual hunched over in his seat. He quickly looked at the photo in the ID and confirmed that it was indeed the man he was approaching. He handed the ID back to the daughter.

The closer he came, the frailer Mr. Borden appeared. His eyes had that glazed over look that Carl had always associated with someone who was not aware of his surroundings. He was glad he had brought that *Request for Assistance* form with him. Clearly his daughter would have to help him with the ballot.

"Daddy, this man has the ballot so you can vote," she said.

Slowly the man turned his head toward Carl. Then in an instant his blank expression was gone. Matthew Borden's eyes focused on the ballot in Carl's hand. He reached out and grabbed the ballot and pen. Suddenly realizing that the *Request for Assistance* form would not be needed, Carl beat a hasty retreat so as to respect Mr. Borden's privacy. From a distance he watched as Mr. Borden marked his ballot with what appeared to be bold, assertive strokes. Carl was deeply moved by the sight.

I wish all those twentysomethings who are too busy to vote could be here to see this, he thought to himself.

Finally Mr. Borden signaled to his daughter that he was done. With a bit of encouragement he placed his ballot in the privacy folder. Carl started to say to Mr. Borden what a privilege it had been to serve him, but already his face had lost its focus and whatever Carl said seemed to have little meaning to him. Carl then led his daughter back into the gym so she could observe her father's ballot being cast. He gave Nancy a quick thumbs up so she could confirm Mr. Borden in the pollbook and led the lady over to the scanner. The scanner took the ballot without a problem. The woman then earnestly thanked him and took her leave.

It was at moments like this, that Carl was proudest to be an election officer.

3

Tuesday, November 4, 8:15 p.m.

"For Governor; Webb 453; Macaulay 445; Stevens 52; write-ins 6; Total 956"

"Right"

For Lieutenant Governor; Patterson 442; Norris 456; write-ins 12; Total 910"

"Correct"

And so it continued. The senior citizen gentleman on the left read the numbers while the young lady on the right confirmed them.

"This is a strange way for me to be spending a Tuesday evening," reflected Cindy Phelps as she waited for her companion to read the next set of numbers, which would hopefully match those that she had already tallied. "Let's see, if it's Tuesday evening, I should be out at some nightspot socializing with my friends. Oh well, it's just a one-time thing."

A one-time thing. That's what her boss had said back in the summer when he announced that all employees at the marketing firm where she worked were "encouraged" to spend a day in "community service." Although she considered herself a Democrat, politics in any form was not really her thing. But then she remembered seeing that brochure at the library on being an election officer. She had filled it out and sent it in, thereby ensuring a check mark in her file next to "community service."

And Cindy had to admit that she had found the day to be oddly satisfying. As by far the youngest officer on the team she had been a bit of a curiosity but everyone had been pleasant. The silver haired chief election officer here at the Cooper precinct, a Republican, had quickly recognized her abilities and had described to her many of the complexities of running a precinct. This had been something of a necessity as the assistant chief, a lady in her late eighties, seemed to have had little function beyond handing out "I Voted" stickers to the voters as they exited.

"Julia really doesn't have it any more," the chief had quietly explained, "but she is a grand old lady with a heart of gold."

Well now at 8:30 p.m. Julia and her heart of gold was in the corner with the other officers as Cindy and the chief were grinding out the numbers on the Statement of Results form. That form was one of the last items to be completed before all the officers, on the job since 5:00 a.m., could call it a night and go home. Actually Cindy had developed a warm spot for Julia who had been very welcoming and the pair had engaged in some nice conversations earlier in the day. She could well understand why the chief was so protective of her.

"Of course, I'll have one last duty," the chief explained. "The chief has to drive the paperwork and supplies in the precinct 'kit' out to the Government Center. It's not a bad drive once you reach the interstate. It's those initial seven miles down Duncan Hill Road that can be a problem."

Cindy understood. Although the apartment where she lived was in the other direction from Cooper Middle School, she had heard stories about the winding Duncan Hill Road with its rises and dips which seemed to have more than its share of accidents, especially at night.

At last the tallying came to an end. It was time for everyone to sign the forms and put this thing to bed. Large envelopes laid out on the table contained the fruits of the thirteen hour day; provisional ballots in one envelope; Statement of Results in another; flash drives from the scanner in yet another; and so on. Seals were affixed to each of the envelopes which were in turn signed by the officers. In some cases two signatures sufficed; in others it was the whole team. At last these envelopes were crammed into the chief's "kit," a sort of suitcase on wheels, and it was time for everyone to say their goodbyes and head on home.

"I hope you don't mind," the chief said to Cindy, "but I wrote in the Chief's Notes that you'd make a splendid chief."

She laughed. "It's not that I don't appreciate the vote of confidence, but this was a one-time thing for me. And besides, even if I were interested, there's no way they would ask a rookie like me."

The chief smiled. "Perhaps. But if the polls are right and Macaulay does win, that will mean a change in parties at the statehouse. Which means that a whole lot of Republican chiefs like me will be replaced by Democrats. You may get that call sooner than you think."

4

NOVEMBER 9

Virginia Politics: Divided Government in Richmond
By J. C. Styles, Washington Herald

Political leaders are analyzing the fallout of Tuesday's election which promises to leave Virginia's government in a state of potential deadlock. At the statewide level Democrats are celebrating the convincing victory of Clinton Macaulay who will be sworn in as the state's 73rd governor next January 14. Even more impressive was Wilbur Norris' overwhelming win by double digit percentage points in the lieutenant governor's race. These coupled with Mildred Foster's victory to the office of Attorney General gave the Democrats a clean sweep in the state wide races.

It is on the legislative side of the government where things seem considerably brighter for the GOP. Republicans maintained control of the House of Delegates by a healthy 65 to 35 seat margin. With the State Senate however things are quite a bit murkier.

Currently all State Senators are in the middle of their four year term and there were no Senate contests on the ballot this past Tuesday. At present each party has twenty Senators. In such situations the lieutenant governor breaks the tie for Senate control. The *complicating factor is that Norris, the lieutenant governor-elect, is also a member of the State Senate representing the 48th Senate district.*

It is anticipated that once Tuesday's results are certified, Norris will resign his Senate seat, thereby requiring a special election which, given the Senate's current composition, will determine which party will win control. With the legislative session scheduled to begin next January 12 and the holiday season looming ahead, it is expected that this special election will occur on Tuesday January 6.

With very little time available for the parties to have a primary, the candidates will most likely be chosen by hastily convened caucuses. Environmental activist Emily Weston has been mentioned as a possible Democratic candidate while businesswoman Jennifer Haley has expressed an interest in making another run on the Republican side. Haley ran a very competitive race against Norris two years ago and insiders say she is eager to try again. It is not known if the Libertarian or Green parties will be fielding candidates.

5

MID-DECEMBER

CARL WAS PUMPED. This was exciting. For the past couple of weeks he had been reading about the upcoming "special election" to be held on January 6. The Norris resignation dictated this hastily called election, an election which would determine which party would control the State Senate. The political spotlight of the state would be on the 48th Senate district. And the Chesterbrook precinct, Carl's precinct, was one of the eight precincts that comprised the 48th.

The truth was that Carl was a self-proclaimed "election nerd." He had majored in computer science at the University of Maryland because "that was where the money is" and he had a reasonably satisfying job at a software firm that paid the bills with something to spare but it was government and politics which were his real passion. The idea of being a facilitator of the democratic process genuinely excited him. Fortunately the state of Virginia with its annual elections punctuated by primaries and occasional "specials" provided him with ample opportunity to exercise his zeal.

And there was the message. The call waiting light had been flashing when he returned from the meeting.

"Carl, this is Rebecca Simpson from the Office of Elections. Could you give me a call at your earliest opportunity?"

This was the call that he had been waiting for. Already his mind was in overdrive. The schools would be closed the next two weeks for the holidays so he would need to call them this week to set up the school visit on the morning of January 5, the day before the election. Eagerly he dialed the number of the Election Office, a number he had long since memorized.

"Office of Elections."

"Hi, is Rebecca Simpson there? This is Carl Marsden returning her call."

"Just a minute."

And then...

"Hi Carl, thanks for getting back so quickly. You know we have this special election coming up on January 6. So we were wondering if you'd be willing to serve as assistant chief at the Chesterbrook precinct."

"*Assistant* chief?"

"Yes, with your background we are confident that you'll do a great job."

"But I've been *chief* officer at Chesterbrook for the past five years."

"I know, but with the change in administrations, the chiefs now all have to be Democrats. Even though the new Democrat governor won't be sworn in until the following week, the Electoral Board decided to make the change effective the beginning of the year."

"So party affiliation is more important than competence?"

"Oh no. Competence is still the driving factor. It's just that the chiefs are now all going to be competent Democrats."

Competent Democrats. Well Nancy Jordan certainly was competent. However Carl had never really pictured her as the leadership type. A bit too quiet and not especially assertive. Still serving under her wouldn't be too bad. They were comfortable with each other and shared a mutual respect. Yes, he was sure they could make it work.

"Carl?"

"Oh sorry, Rebecca. What is it?"

"Do you accept the appointment?"

"Absolutely. I'm looking forward to it."

"Wonderful. You'll need to attend one of the meetings at the Government Center for chiefs and assistant chiefs. They will be Monday and Tuesday evenings, December 29 and 30 at 7:00 p.m. Let us know which one you'll be attending."

"The 29th works for me. I'll be there. Thank you, Rebecca."

Putting down the phone, Carl felt rather let down. He understood that election duty was a one day thing. Serving one time in no way guaranteed another assignment. Still he took a great deal of pride in the way he had managed his precinct and couldn't help but feel a certain amount of injustice with the situation. Of course he knew that the tradition was that the chief was of the same party as the sitting governor. But this had never been strictly followed in the past. To quote a popular movie, it had been more of a "guideline" than a strict "rule." Indeed a few of the times that Carl had served as chief had been during a Democratic administration. So this new emphasis on party affiliation was a bit unsettling.

Still at least he'd be part of the action. And ultimately it was the process of democracy that this was all about and Carl did feel deeply about that. Yes, he would shove aside whatever disappointment he might have and work with Nancy to make it happen.

6

LATE DECEMBER

IT WAS ABOUT a quarter to seven, Monday evening December 29 when Carl walked into the conference room at the Government Center where the meeting was to take place. He had just been issued his "chief's manual," a loose-leaf binder that contained the step-by-step instructions to be followed on Election Day. He already knew much of the book by heart but he still made the effort to review its contents before each election.

At 36 years of age, Carl had always been something of the "boy wonder" among the chiefs. Most of the chiefs were older, frequently much older, with retired and semi-retired individuals in great abundance. Now however (and perhaps it was only his imagination), it seemed that with the party turnover, the chiefs had a somewhat "younger look." In fact, one of them, a rather attractive young lady with long brown hair who had already taken a seat in the front row, looked like she belonged at a college frat party rather than here.

Carl looked around the room for Nancy Jordan. He hoped that she would be attending this meeting so they could do some planning but she did not appear to be here.

I guess she will be at the Tuesday meeting, he thought as he took his seat.

He opened his chief's manual and looked for the insert, the roster page that gave the names and phone numbers of the "team" that he would be working with on Election Day. Finding the page on the inside sleeve, Carl gave a quiet gasp.

Nancy's name was not listed. Instead the name given as chief was "Cynthia Phelps." Carl racked his brain trying remember the various Democratic election officers he had worked with over the past few years but try as he might, no "Cynthia Phelps" came to mind.

He glanced at the woman who was seated to his immediate left. She appeared to be in her mid-eighties and was half dozing in her chair. Carl looked quickly at the roster sheet in her hand. It identified her as Julia Hopkins, chief election officer for the Cooper precinct.

I hope Cooper has a strong assistant chief, he thought, thankful at least that this lady did not appear to be Cynthia Phelps.

An older African American man sat on the other side of him.

"Hi Milton, so this will be your show next Tuesday," Carl offered.

"So it appears," responded Milton. "All eight precincts are on my normal route. Still this should be a fairly easy one, I think."

Carl agreed. Milton was one of the "rovers." Rovers were seasonal employees, generally former chiefs, who on Election Day drove a preassigned "route" of precincts. They generally visited each precinct twice on Election Day and provided the chiefs on an "as needed" basis with extra supplies, technical assistance, advice, and/or encouragement. Milton had been Carl's rover ever since he started working at the Chesterbrook precinct. In truth Milton had never really had to assist him with anything beyond occasionally providing forms when the original supply ran out. Still

Carl always enjoyed Milton's visits to the precinct as he would let everyone know what was happening in the "outside world" (i.e. the other precincts).

It looked like the meeting was about to start but Carl did have one question for Milton.

"Do you know who Cynthia Phelps is?" he asked pointing to the roster.

"She's a new chief," replied Milton. He pulled out one of his papers which gave the names and backgrounds of those chiefs and assistants who were new to their jobs.

"Let's see," Milton said studying his sheet. "She has never been a chief and never been an assistant. She has been an officer once; last November, in fact."

"That's not much of a resume."

"I assume her chief recommended her. Perhaps I might recognize her by sight but I'm afraid the name doesn't ring a bell. I'll make a point to visit Chesterbrook early in the day and you have my number if I'm needed sooner."

"Good Evening everyone," came the voice over the microphone. "For those of you who don't know me, I am Grace Fields, Election Manager for our county. First let me thank you all for agreeing to be chiefs and assistant chiefs for this special election coming so soon after the holidays. I do have one initial assignment for each of you. The long range weather forecast suggests that a 'precipitation event' is not out of the question for next Tuesday so I ask each of you to petition the deity of your choice to 'Please keep it dry on Tuesday.'"

Nervous laughter greeted the request. Most in the room had not really thought that far in advance.

Most of the meeting covered items that Carl was familiar with. Grace did emphasize the heightened media attention on this race that apparently would decide which political party would control the State Senate. She also emphasized the need to keep the partisan poll watchers from overstepping their bounds while maintaining cordial relations. After about an hour she had all the chiefs and assistant chiefs rise to take the election oath, the same oath that they would be administering to the officers on Election Day.

"I do solemnly swear (or affirm) that I will perform the duties for this election according to law and the best of my ability and that I will studiously endeavor to prevent fraud, deceit, and abuse in conducting this election."

At this point the meeting was adjourned. The chiefs still had one more task which was to pick up his/her kit of supplies which for this election only, included the same two-way radio that the rovers used on a regular basis. These radios would facilitate communication between the chiefs and either the rovers or the Government Center. For the first time in years, Carl did not need to pick up those items and with a certain bittersweet feeling he departed from the Government Center.

7

TUESDAY, DECEMBER 30

"H ELLO"

"Nancy, this is Carl Marsden."

"*(chuckling)* I had a feeling you might be calling."

"Is everything OK? Are you and Hank all right?"

"We're just fine. Thank you."

"I missed you at the chiefs meeting. I was hoping to be serving under you next Tuesday."

"It's nice of you to say that Carl. Hank and I will be in Florida all of January. We hooked into a time share at West Palm Beach. We are now officially snowbirds."

"*(with mock indignation)*...and leaving me to break in a new chief. Her name is Cynthia Phelps. Any idea who she might be."

"Can't say that I do. I've been working with the same folks as you have these past few years."

"Milton says she's never been a chief or an assistant. And only once as an officer."

"Well whatever may be, please remember that she is in charge. Carl, you're a great chief and good guy but you can be...oh how shall I say it...a bit intense. Be supportive but let her lead. They would not have appointed her if she wasn't any good. And enjoy that fact that for once, you are not ultimately responsible."

"Yes, you're right of course. Well you have a great New Year and a wonderful time in Florida."

"Happy New Year to you, too. And good luck on Tuesday."

8

FRIDAY, JANUARY 2

CARL DID NOT expect to get a call from his chief right away; certainly not before New Year's Day had come and gone. The remaining festivities of the holiday season consumed most of his time although he did manage to begin reviewing his manual. He also scanned with interest the names of the remaining officers on the roster.

Pam and Jerry Blevens, both Democrats, were an older married couple that had served with him for years. They were both good reliable workers although Jerry could get somewhat flustered under pressure.

Also on the list was Theodore McDougald, an Independent. Carl had to smile when he thought of him. Theodore had been on his team the first time that Carl had been chief at Chesterbrook. He was rather elderly with a shy demeanor and unassuming personality. Carl immediately assigned him the position of greeter, a job that promised not to be taxing as the turnout for this particular election, a primary, promised to be light. He carefully explained the duties of the position to him. Theodore did not seem sure that he was up to it but said he would give it a try.

For the first few hours Theodore performed his duties with diligence and growing enthusiasm and eventually Carl started giving him more challenging assignments. With each "promotion," Theodore was initially hesitant, fearful that he was not up to the job, but with Carl's careful instruction and encouragement he was able to work up to it. By the end of the day Theodore had proved himself to be a solid contributor to the team. Ever since, Carl had regarded him as one of his true "success stories"; the additional result being that Carl was always ready to give a new officer "the benefit of the doubt" no matter how unpromising he might initially seem to be.

The remaining two officers were unfamiliar to Carl. They were listed as Millicent LaGrande and Jeffrey Hynes, both Republicans.

So that's seven officers counting the chief and himself, thought Carl. Probably enough for an election with a very simple ballot. The great unknown was voter participation. Normally a special election coming right after the holidays would mean a very light turnout but with control of the State Senate at stake, there had been a fair amount of publicity. Turnout could be higher than one might think. Still with seven officers we should be OK.

By Friday January 2, Carl was getting antsy. Why hadn't his chief called? Finally the wait got the better of him. If she wasn't going to initiate contact then he had to. Normally when he served as chief he would initially try to reach his officers by their home phone. Only after failing to connect a few times would he resort to the cell phone. He did not want to call an officer when they were at work or in their car if he could help it.

Carl looked at the roster and saw that there was both a cell phone and work phone listed for Cynthia Phelps but no home phone. Under the circumstances he had no choice. He dialed her cell phone number. After four rings, a recorded message came on.

"Hi, this is Cindy. I'm out and about right now so just leave a message and I'll get back to you. Have a great day."

"Cynthia, this is Carl Marsden. I'm the assistant chief at the Chesterbrook precinct where you are chief for next Tuesday's election. We probably should talk soon. Hopefully you've been able to contact the Chesterbrook Elementary School to arrange a time for us to meet at the school on Monday so we can examine the cart and talk to the custodian. And also hopefully you've started to call the officers. You can reach me at either my home phone or cell with the numbers on the roster sheet. Talk to you soon."

OK, I think I said it all, thought Carl as he put down the phone. *I don't want to be too preachy. That voice on the recording sounded awful young, though. I sure hope the electoral office knew what they were doing when they made the appointment.*

And with that Carl went back to reading the manual.

9

SUNDAY, JANUARY 4

All Eyes Turn to Eight Precincts
By J. C. Styles, Washington Herald, Sunday edition

In only two days the political eyes of Virginia will focus on eight precincts located here in the northern part of the state. Voters will go to the polls to select the next State Senator for Virginia's 48th senate district which will in turn determine which party controls the State Senate for the upcoming legislative term.

The choice will be between Democrat environmentalist Emily Weston and Republican businesswoman Jennifer Haley to fill the vacancy created by the resignation of Lieutenant Governor-elect Wilbur Norris. The resignation of Norris has given the Republicans a temporary 20-19 majority in the State Senate. A Weston victory would create a 20-20 tie which would then be broken by Lieutenant Governor Norris, while a Haley win would expand the Republican control to a 21-19 margin.

With a relatively light turnout expected, observers are having a difficult time handicapping the race. Norris' narrow victory over Haley two years ago suggests that this could be a very close contest. By far the largest precinct in the district is the heavily populated

Manchester precinct with over 3,500 voters. Manchester usually gives the Democrats a healthy majority as does its neighboring Seneca Grove precinct. In contrast the precincts of Wallingford, Danby, Easthampton, and Hagerman to varying degrees generally support the Republicans. Some analysts believe that it might all come down to the two northernmost precincts, Cooper and Chesterbrook where the parties have been fairly evenly divided in recent years.

"We are putting on an all court press," declared Democratic Party County Chair Brian "Biff" Logan. "We will have poll watchers at all the precincts who will be diligently looking for any signs of voter intimidation, a common tactic of Republican operatives." Republican Party chair, Karen McIntosh echoed similar sentiments only emphasizing the Republican Party's commitment to "stamp out voter fraud."

As always caught in the middle of this political rancor is county Election Manager Grace Fields who is predicting a very orderly, well-run election.

"Our chiefs and assistants have been thoroughly briefed; the voting locations have been duly notified; and the precinct carts have been shipped from the warehouse to the precincts. Our teams of officers will be ready to greet the voters when polls open at 6 a.m. Tuesday for voting."

Fields indicated that the number of absentee ballots received at the Government Center thus far has been "quite small" and that "as always" absentee ballots will be counted Tuesday evening at the same time that the precincts are tallying their results.

A potential complicating factor in Tuesday's contest is the weather. Although the snowstorm that was once feared will probably not take place, meteorologists are still holding out the possibility of a "precipitation event", beginning as rain Tuesday afternoon and later turning to "something else." Fields declined to say whether *such an event might cause the polls to extend their 7:00 p.m. closing time.*

"We are getting way ahead of ourselves on this," she declared. "Voters need to simply be aware that the polls will be open on Tuesday, as always here in Virginia, from 6:00 a.m. to 7:00 p.m."

10

SUNDAY AFTERNOON

"HELLO"

"Hello, Is Cynthia Phelps there?"

"Speaking."

"Cynthia, this is Carl Marsden, your assistant chief for Tuesday's election."

A pause, followed by:

"Oh, hi."

She's not exactly bubbling with enthusiasm, thought Carl.

"I was wondering how everything is looking for Tuesday."

"I think we're in pretty good shape."

"Have you called your officers yet?"

Another pause.

"I'm just about to."

Carl couldn't quite comprehend what he was hearing. She must have had her list of officers since Tuesday at least. And here it was Sunday and she still hadn't even begun to contact them.

"How about the school? We need to go over there sometime tomorrow to check things out."

"I know. I'll be giving them a call tomorrow morning to set things up. I'll call you when I know the time."

"You mean you haven't talked to them yet?"

Yet, another pause.

"You do know that the schools have been closed the last two weeks for the holiday."

"Yeah but you were appointed back in—no, I'm sorry. Never mind."

An awkward silence. Carl couldn't help but remember how poised he was to contact the school back in mid-December when he thought he was going to be chief. And here she had let the whole thing slide. Something just wasn't quite right. Suddenly he felt the need to ask,

"Cynthia, have you done this before?"

"It's Cindy, and yes, I have done this before."

"I'm sorry, I just want this—"

"Look, I served last November at Cooper. It was good. I'm reading the manual. It's all good."

Her icy tone signaled an end to the topic.

"OK, then I guess I'll look forward to your call tomorrow. I plan to take off tomorrow so I'm pretty much available all day. Just call me on the cell."

"Sounds good. See you tomorrow. Bye."

"Good bye."

11

Sunday afternoon, a few minutes later

*W*ELL, CARL THOUGHT upon hanging up; *that did not go as well as I had hoped.*

Carl had planned to reassure Cynthia (check, Cindy) that he was very familiar with the facilities and staff at Chesterbrook and would be glad to share his knowledge with her. In addition he had drawn up what he thought might be a good distribution of assignments among the officers for the setup and the first two hours based on his knowledge of their strengths and limitations. The opening for such a conversation had unfortunately never materialized. Carl would attempt to have that discussion with her tomorrow. In the meantime he wasn't sure if she was indifferent or hostile or what but he definitely felt uneasy about the whole situation.

At the other end, the conversation had given Cindy an unsettling feeling as well. The simple reality, she admitted to herself, was that she had let the time pass by and was now trying to catch up. In fact she had only started to read the manual that morning.

She had not given it a whole lot of thought when Rebecca from the elections office had called and asked her to be chief. Her company had just announced that the "day of community service" had become an annual requirement so this seemed like a quick and easy way of getting it out of the way so early in the year. And being the "chief" might even look good on her resume. Sure, she'd do it. She had sort of enjoyed it in November and how much more difficult could being a chief be?

Then came the holidays with all its shopping, parties, gift giving, and family events, which were in turn followed by even more parties (and one horrendous hangover). Suddenly here she was two days before the election and way behind where she ought to be. The fact that her assistant chief appeared to be a bit of a pompous jerk did not improve her mood.

"Still," she reflected. *"I made the commitment and I need to follow through. But this is the last time. After Tuesday I'm done."*

12

SUNDAY EVENING

"**H**ELLO, Is CYNTHIA Phelps there?"
(*Oh no! Not another one.*)

"This is Cindy. Can I help you?"

"Hello, this is Milton Ayres, your rover for this Tuesday's election. I was wondering if you need anything."

Like a new assistant chief, Cindy thought.

"Well I've called all my people. They're all confirmed except one. Jeffrey Hynes says he can't make it."

"So that puts you at six. You should be OK with that. Still you might want to call the Government Center tomorrow morning. I think all the backups are committed but you never know."

"Also I'll be calling the school tomorrow morning to set things up for later in the day. I think my assistant chief was a bit miffed that I hadn't contacted them sooner."

"That would have been kind of difficult with the schools not in session the past two weeks."

Well at least someone understands.

"Any suggestions for tomorrow's meeting at the school?"

"Not really. The people at Chesterbrook are generally cooperative. I wish all the schools were that way. You can pretty much depend on them to deliver what they say. And don't be afraid to rely on your assistant chief. Carl has done this for a number of years and knows it quite well."

"Just out of curiosity. Am I the only rookie chief serving in this election?"

"The only one. The others were all chiefs back when the Democrats were in power the last time. But don't worry. You've got a good team behind you and a cooperative school. Just follow the manual step-by-step and you'll be fine. Still if you'd like, I can arrange for Chesterbrook to be my first visit at 5:00 a.m. Tuesday morning for the opening."

Cindy readily agreed. Yes, she would appreciate Milton's presence at the ungodly hour of 5:00 a.m. when each of the eight precinct chiefs would be on the line to get their precincts up and functioning by six. They exchanged a few pleasantries before saying good night. She did feel a bit better after hanging up. Perhaps this wouldn't be too painful after all.

13

MONDAY MORNING, JANUARY 5, 9:00 A.M.

"**H**ELLO"

"Hello Carl, this is Cindy Phelps. I've talked to the school and we have an appointment to meet the assistant principal at four o'clock this afternoon. After that we can inspect the cart and hopefully set up the room. We are in the gym."

"The gym? I think you mean the library. We get the gym in November when school is not in session but for primaries and specials like this, with school in session, they always move us to the library."

"The person I talked to said it was the gym."

"Are you sure?"

For a moment Cindy was tempted to answer with *"No Carl, I just made it up about the gym to annoy you."* However she fought back the temptation and replied with a simple,

"Yes I am sure."

"Hmm...OK. I tell you what. Why don't we meet in front of the school at about 3:45? I'd like to share with you some of my thoughts before we go in about the precinct, room setup, and our team of officers."

"OK. Sounds good." (*I just can't wait to hear your thoughts.*)

"Oh and one other thing. From my experience if we really are in the gym, then they probably won't let us set up the room on Monday afternoon. That's because they generally have youth basketball on Monday night. So we will need to provide a diagram of what we want and the a.m. custodian will set it up for us."

Now it was Cindy's turn to be concerned.

"That sounds rather risky. At Cooper they let us set up the day before. Aren't we leaving ourselves at the mercy of some nameless, faceless custodian?"

"She is not nameless; she is not faceless. Her name is Tess and I have worked with her for several election cycles."

"But if she is the a.m. custodian we won't even see her this afternoon."

"I know. It would have been better if we could have met with them in the morning when Tess was at the school. I really don't know the p.m. custodians at all. I've never even seen them. But I'm sure we'll find someone who can pass the diagram on to Tess. Look Cindy, I've worked with these people for years. They're good. If we tell them what we need, they'll deliver."

"All right, if you say so. I'll see you then at 3:45."

"Right on. See you then."

14

Monday afternoon, 3:45 p.m.

CINDY ARRIVED IN her two seater sports car at 3:45 on the dot. She got out of the car, armed with her chief's manual, and proceeded to walk toward the front door of the school. There seated on the bench was a man who appeared to be in his mid-thirties, presumably Carl. Cindy was a bit surprised. She expected to find some sort of nerdy dweeb. Fortunately Carl appeared to be refreshingly normal, even attractive in a bookish sort of way. Not exactly her type but still…

Determined to put any misunderstanding behind them, Cindy put on her most radiant smile.

"Mr. Marsden, I presume," she said offering an outstretched hand. "We meet at last."

Getting to his feet, Carl shook her hand.

"Ah, yes," he replied. "I think I remember you from the chiefs meeting. First row if I recall."

Then added, "Did you bring the kit?"

"The kit?"

"Yes you need the key from the kit to open the precinct cart. Also the paperwork inside the kit has the serial numbers to be compared with the scanner."

Oh crap, she thought. She had read somewhere that she needed to bring the kit with her to the precinct on Monday but had forgotten.

"It's back at my apartment, I'm afraid," she stammered, feeling like a delinquent school girl who had forgotten her homework. "Look, it's only five minutes away. I'll go back and get it."

Carl frowned, a look of disappointment on his face.

"We really do need that kit to do our job," he said in an almost lecturing tone. "But let's go ahead and have our meeting with the staff. Once that's done and we have established where the precinct cart is, you can go back for the kit."

Carl then opened his manual and took out a piece of paper with a diagram on it. They both sat down.

"I've taken the liberty to sketch how I think it might work. Here's the entrance to the gym," he said pointing to his sketch.

"We can put the Electronic Pollbooks, otherwise known as the EPBs, immediately inside the door. The poll watchers table will be directly behind. Once we check them in at the Pollbook table, they will receive their ballot cards and proceed to the ballot table over here," he said pointing to another part of the diagram.

"Then after getting their ballots they will proceed to the privacy booths that we will set up on the table here to mark their ballots. Then they insert their completed ballots in the scanner over here and finally exit out the same door they entered."

Carl continued to point at various parts of his diagram as he was speaking.

"Nice and neat. We'll have the cart locked in the corner where we can store the ballots and ladies handbags. A table on the side will have the 'Create Ballot' machine for the handicapped voters. We will have a chief's table over there where you can park your various forms and stuff. And a table in the far corner for our personal things. And that should be that."

Carl looked up with an expression that oozed with self-satisfaction.

All during Carl's monologue, Cindy sat silently seething. He was treating her like some brainless nitwit who needed to be molded into his version of what a chief election officer should be. Well he may be experienced and smart and all that other stuff but damn it, Cindy was the chief and unless she did something real quick to show it, she was afraid she would lose all control of the situation.

She carefully removed a sheet of paper from her manual and began to construct her own diagram.

"I'm not sure having the EPBs just inside the door is the best plan," she said thoughtfully. "That will push any line at all back into the hall. The gym is a large room. We can move the EPBs back into the gym and keep the line inside."

"Not really," said Carl smugly. "The power outlets are by the door. The EPBs require power. We don't want long extension cords all over the place."

Not all over the place, thought Cindy. *Just around your neck.*

"Surely the outlets by the door are not the only ones in the gym," she said.

"There are some by the far wall but we don't want people walking the length of the gym."

"Why not? They have already walked all the way in from the parking lot and down the hall. What's a few more steps?"

Cindy then looked across at Carl's diagram.

"What's that other door?" she asked, pointing at his diagram.

"That's just a side door that leads out to the side of the school. We never use it."

"Is it that door over there?" asked Cindy pointing to a side door she had passed after leaving the parking lot.

"That's the one."

"Well," she said finishing her diagram, "we can have the voters leave by that door. That will put them right by the parking lot when they exit saving them any extra steps they might have taken by walking the length of the gym. Also it avoids the confusion that can occur when voters enter and exit by the same door."

"But we've never done it that way."

"Maybe it's time for a change."

They looked at each other for what seemed an eternity but in reality was only a few seconds.

Carl broke the silence. "Look let's table our differences on this until we are actually in the gym. I just want to go over with you my thoughts on the team members."

"Fire away."

"Pam Blevens is probably our best officer. She's capable, personable, calm under pressure, and not afraid of technology. During the setup I would have her work on getting the EPBs up and running. Then for the first shift have her on the EPBs. I can work with her on both fronts. We work well together. Her husband Jerry is also reasonably capable; he should work with you to get the scanner up and running. After that he can man the ballot table. He is good at counting out the packages of ballots as we need to use them."

"Theodore is a marvelous old gentleman," continued Carl, "but he needs a certain amount of direction. I would have him put up the signs. Once the polls open he will either be the greeter or work the scanner. Later in the day when the lines ease up he can do some of the more challenging things. This leaves the two Republicans, Millicent LaGrande and Jeffrey Hynes. I don't know them at all. We'll have to size them up when they arrive."

"Oh, I forgot to mention. Hynes isn't coming."

"Can we get a replacement?"

"I called the Government Center this morning. All the replacement officers are spoken for."

"Well maybe if you had called everyone last week—" Carl started to say but stopped. There was no point harping on her slow start since there was nothing they could do about it anyway.

"Six should be enough," said Cindy. "But regardless that's all we've got. The Government Center said that there just aren't many people so soon after the holidays who are up for this election."

"Are you sure you're up for it?"

Carl could not believe what he had just said. Cindy's slowness to get the ball rolling, her simple mistakes like leaving the kit at home, her apparent determination to reconfigure the gym, and mostly Carl's lingering disappointment on not being chief had caused him to blurt out something completely inappropriate.

Cindy said nothing but the intensity of her eyes boring in on Carl reflected the cold anger that she felt.

He tried to repair the damage.

"Look, I'm sorry. That was completely out of line. I apologize."

She continued to be silent.

"Look, we're closing in on 4:00 p.m.," he continued. "Let's resolve our issue concerning the gym layout and then we can go inside to meet the assistant principal."

With deliberate calmness Cindy asked, "May I see your diagram?"

Carl handed it to her.

Cindy studied the diagram for a few seconds and then ever so slowly closed her fingers around the paper, squeezing it into a crumpled ball. She then returned the ball to Carl.

"Issue resolved," she said softly.

15

MONDAY AFTERNOON, 4:00 P.M.

T HEY ENTERED THE school in stony silence and proceeded to the school office. As they were entering the office, the secretary looked up from her desk. Her expression showed that she recognized Carl from earlier elections. However before they could actually verbalize a greeting, Cindy stepped forward, partially blocking Carl from view, and saying with as much cheerful assertiveness as she could muster,

"Hi. I'm Cindy Phelps, chief election officer for tomorrow's election. I'm here with my assistant to talk with your assistant principal about tomorrow. Could you let her know that we are here?"

"Yes, I think Mrs. Martin is expecting you," said the secretary. "I'll go back and tell her you're here."

"Thank you so much," said Cindy, a bright smile on her face.

You're quite the charmer when you want to be, thought Carl.

A woman of about Carl's age emerged from one of the doors and approached them.

"Hi Carl," she said. "You folks keep springing these elections on us. Great to see you again. You're breaking in a new assistant chief I see."

"Hi, I'm Michelle Martin," she said, turning to Cindy.

Then back to Carl, "Let's go back to my office and discuss things."

Cindy gave Carl a hard stare as if to say "Why didn't you correct her?" Carl merely shrugged and smiled.

Upon entering Mrs. Martin's office, Cindy spoke up, determined that this misunderstanding go no further.

"Actually for this election I'm the chief officer and Carl's the assistant," she said trying to apply graciousness and firmness in equal measure.

Mrs. Martin's face registered a bit of surprise. "Oh really?"

"It's a party thing," interjected Carl. "The change of administrations in Richmond resulted in the modifying of our roles."

"I see," replied Mrs. Martin still not quite comprehending. "Well I'm sure the two of you will pull it off splendidly."

"Oh yes," said Cindy. "We're very close."

"I was surprised to hear that you're giving us the gym," said Carl. "Usually when school's in session we are relegated to the much smaller library."

"Normally we would have," said Mrs. Martin. "But we have some mandated standardized testing tomorrow which will cause all the gym classes to be canceled. So you luck out on that score. The bad news is that there is some youth basketball tonight so you will not be able to set up right now. However if you give Tess your setup diagram, she'll have it done by the time you arrive tomorrow at 5:00 a.m."

"We do have our diagram," said Cindy, flashing a quick smile in Carl's direction. "Can you make sure Tess gets it?"

Mrs. Martin smiled. "Actually Tess is at the school right now. Carl, when she heard you were scheduled to meet with us this afternoon she insisted on coming in so that everything would be exactly the way you want it."

Now it was Carl's turn to beam.

They talked for a few minutes more, mostly about the need for security with the school in session. It was critical that the incoming voters be restricted to only the hallway leading to the gym as well as the gym itself; and no wandering off by voters to other parts of the school would be tolerated. For once Cindy and Carl were in complete agreement.

"Now I believe Tess is down in the gym," said Mrs. Martin. "Let's go down there and see if we can find her."

Together they left the office area and walked down the hall to the gym. Upon entering the gym, a slight Asian woman of indeterminate age in a custodian's uniform gave out a cry of recognition.

"Carl!" she cried. "So good to see you again."

She gave Carl a big hug. Then looking at Cindy she added. "I see you have a new assistant. What happened to Miss Nancy?"

The next few minutes were spent discussing Nancy Jordan's Florida vacation along with Carl and Tess's respective holiday seasons. Somewhere in there, Cindy managed to interject that she, not Carl, was the chief for this election but she wasn't really sure if Tess got the message. Mrs. Martin said her goodbyes and left.

Cindy handed Tess her diagram.

"This is how we would like the room set up," she said. "Can this be done by 5:00 a.m.?"

Tess frowned, looking at the paper.

"This is not the way we usually do it," she said looking up at Carl.

For a few seconds, an uneasy silence pervaded the gym. Tess looked at Carl, waiting for direction. Cindy looked at Carl, hoping for support.

Finally he said, "We're trying something new Tess. I think this should be OK."

"Very good Carl. If you want it, that's the way it will be," said Tess, a smile returning to her face.

Cindy breathed a little easier. She was about to quietly express her appreciation to Carl for his support, however grudgingly given, when he abruptly turned around and started walking to the far end of the gym. She hurried to keep up with him.

"What in blazes are you doing?" she asked as they neared the far wall. "Oh and thank you for your support back there. I know it wasn't easy for you."

"You won't be thanking me tomorrow if we don't make sure of one little thing today," he said kneeling down in front of the wall sockets at the base of the wall. Then he pulled a small nightlight out of his pocket.

"I've never used these outlets before," he said. "These are the wall sockets you want to use for the EPBs. We need to make sure they work."

He inserted the nightlight into each of the outlets in turn, cupping his hands about the light to simulate darkness. In each instance the light came on.

"The devil is in the details," he said looking up at Cindy. He was tempted to add, *"and if you won't do it then I must"* but he held back, thinking that the point had been made.

Cindy for her part said nothing. Internally she had to admit, *"You do know your stuff, you pompous jerk."*

They crossed back over to the other side where Tess was still standing.

"Carl, would you like to see where the cart and the scanner are?" asked Tess.

Cindy was briefly tempted to scream at Tess, *"I'm the chief, not Carl,"* but quickly thought better of it. Carl was the man as far as Tess was concerned and nothing she said would change that. In fact she was beginning to feel just a bit ashamed of herself. She was obsessing too much about this turf war with Carl and not the real goal that they all shared of running a smooth election.

Tess led them to a closed door off the main corridor. She took out her fully loaded key ring and produced, as if by magic, the correct one. She unlocked the door and led them into a large closet which contained, among an ocean of school supplies, the optical scanner sitting astride a large black bin on wheels along with a long metal cart, also on wheels. The cart had stenciled on its side "Chesterbrook."

"These were delivered several days ago and they have been stored here under lock and key ever since," she explained. "I'll be wheeling them out into the gym overnight according to your diagram when I set things up. For now they will stay here. Stay as long as you like to examine things; just remember to close the door when you are done. It locks automatically. Now if you don't need anything else, I'm going home. I'll see you both tomorrow at 5:00 a.m."

They said their goodbyes. Cindy was somewhat heartened that Tess had said "see you both."

"I guess this is where I go back home and get that kit," she said.

"I'll wait for you right here," replied Carl.

The roundtrip took about fifteen minutes. When she returned, pulling her suitcase on wheels, referred to as the "kit," she found Carl leaning against the wall reading his manual. She couldn't help but wonder, *"What do you do with your life when there isn't an election?"*

The examination of the cart and scanner went rather smoothly. They were both a bit drained from their bickering and neither wanted to risk touching the other's hot spots. The result was a guarded, polite, formality that they used to get through their tasks.

With wire cutters from the kit, Cindy cut open the plastic seal that wrapped around the handle of the cart. She then used the key from her kit to unlock the cart door. The cart was properly stocked. There were the promised two Electronic Pollbooks (EPBs), a bag of "peripheral" accessories for the EPBs, two "Create Ballot" machines for the handicapped voters, six of the so called real estate signs with their wire frames, a large canvas bag filled with a plethora of signs and forms, a smaller bag with power cords and extension cords, some cardboard privacy booths, and a few other miscellaneous things. All there.

Next with Carl's guidance, Cindy pulled out the Statement of Results form from her kit and verified that the scanner's serial number matched the number on the form.

The last thing they verified was the box of printed ballots. Chesterbook had approximately 2,400 voters. Even with the increased media attention, most observers felt the turnout would be low, 10%, maybe 15%. The brown box of printed ballots read "Chesterbrook; 6 packages of 100 ballots each."

"That's 600 ballots," observed Carl. "Which means we're good for a 25% turnout. I would say that's sufficient."

Cindy nodded although in truth she did not have the slightest idea if that was sufficient or not.

At that point they had done all that could be done. There was a log sheet in the sleeve on the inside of the door of the cart that they both signed. The cart door was closed and locked and a new seal wrapped through the door handle.

"I guess that's it," said Carl.

"I guess that's it," confirmed Cindy.

They walked out of the school together in silence, Cindy pulling her kit on wheels behind her. They reached Carl's car first.

"Well I'll be seeing you tomorrow at 5:00 a.m.," he said.

She gave him a slight smile, which seemed to reflect tired resignation rather than joyous anticipation.

"I wouldn't miss it."

16

Monday afternoon, 5:30 p.m.

From: Grace Fields, Election Manager
To: All chiefs, Special Election January 6
Here are a few points to review before tomorrow's Special Election:

1. We are hearing rumors that one or both of the political parties are going to try to "test the system" tomorrow. What form such a "test" might take is open to speculation but it is vital that chief election officers, assistant chiefs, and their teams abide by all the rules and laws to the fullest extent.

2. For this election all chefs have been issued a two-way radio. These radios, normally given only to the rovers, will facilitate communications between the chiefs and the Command Center. We have designated four times during the day when such communications are mandatory. They are:

    a. 6:00 a.m. - chiefs will radio the Command Center to confirm that the precinct is open and ready to process voters.

b. 10:00 a.m. - chiefs will communicate the number of votes cast so far to the Command Center.

c. 2:00 p.m. - chiefs will communicate the number of votes cast so far to the Command Center.

d. After 7:00 p.m. - chiefs will communicate election results for their precinct to Command Center.

3. Chiefs are reminded that these two-way radios operate on an open frequency and calls can be monitored by anyone with a radio. Hence all communications which are sensitive and/or site specific should be handled by cell phone.

4. The two candidates in this election reside in the Manchester and Chesterbrook precincts respectively. It is anticipated that each will be voting sometime early in the morning. They will probably be accompanied by TV cameras and reporters. Chiefs are to provide them every courtesy without disrupting the precinct or the other voters. All chiefs should review the section on dealing with Press/TV in your manual.

5. The Office of Elections has granted permission to members of Brazil's House of Representatives and South Korea's National Assembly to observe the electoral process at the Chesterbrook and Danby precincts respectively. Chiefs are to extend them every courtesy while ensuring that their visit does not interfere with the voters and election officers performing their respective roles.

6. Chiefs are reminded that both political parties are most anxious to hear the results of this election. Chiefs should radio in the results as soon as they are known. Chiefs should not wait until all the paperwork is done to complete this task.

7. Weather forecasts indicate that a precipitation event will probably occur in the area starting around the 3:00 p.m. time frame. What form this precipitation might take has not been specified. Barring unforeseen events chiefs are to adhere to the regular closing schedules as established by law and county practice. Polls will close precisely at 7:00 p.m.

8. Chiefs are to return their kits with completed forms and other materials in the correct envelopes/boxes to the Government Center tomorrow evening no later than 10:00 p.m. and ideally by 9:00 p.m. This is a rather straightforward election and the closing activities should not take that long.

9. The Command Center will be open for business starting at 5:00 a.m. to handle any questions that might come up. It will remain open until all precincts have radioed in their final results at the end of the day. In addition our rover, Milton Ayres will be circulating among the precincts. He will have additional supplies and is just a phone call away.

Finally we wish all the chiefs, assistant chiefs, and election officers the very best of luck tomorrow. We have excellent teams of officers at each of our precincts and we are confident the day will be a rousing success.

17(a)

Monday Evening

It was 9:00 p.m. and Milton had just completed his preparation for the following morning. His supplies were in his car and his lunch and snacks had been prepared.

Mentally he went over the precincts he would be covering. Each precinct had its own unique quirks and challenges. Mostly though he was concerned about some of the election officers. The office had experienced an unusually difficult time in recruiting officers to serve in this election. Coming so soon after the holidays, many of the regulars had decided to "pass" on this one. Interestingly enough Milton's primary concern was not with the chiefs but the assistant chiefs.

Ideally, the Republicans who had served as chiefs in November would be serving as assistant chiefs here in January. However this was not to be the case in three of his precincts. Seneca Grove, Hagerman, and Cooper all had rookie assistant chiefs, each of whom had to be "talked into" accepting the appointment. Now this would not be a problem if the precinct had a strong chief who could mentor the assistant even as he/she kept the precinct on an even keel. Milton was reasonably confident with the chiefs at Seneca Grove and Hagerman. Cooper was another story.

Which brings me to the chiefs, he thought.

Seven of the eight precincts would be led by persons who had been chiefs when Democrats had last been in power. The one exception was Chesterbrook where Cindy Phelps, a complete novice would be in charge. At first he had not known who she was but late in their conversation she mentioned that she had been at Cooper the previous fall and Milton immediately recalled the young lady who the chief had raved about.

And of course she would be backed by Carl Marsden as assistant chief and Carl was one of the best. From her words during their phone conversation, Milton sensed there might be a bit of friction between the two but he was confident they could work it out. Milton had committed to her that he would be on hand at 5:00 a.m. when they would get things started but it was a commitment that Milton now wished he had not made.

"Which leaves me with Cooper," he pondered. Julia Hopkins was practically an institution. She had served the county as an election officer at Cooper for over thirty years and as chief for more than twenty. With her intelligence, resourcefulness, poise, dignity, all laced with a sense of humor, she had guided the Cooper precinct through numerous demographic shifts, county and school personnel changes, and generations of voting equipment. Then four years ago when the Republicans won the statehouse it was decided that a member of the GOP would be chief and Julia would be the assistant.

Now Milton couldn't be sure of this since a precinct's assistant chief was usually not his focus but it seemed that Julia had sunk bit-by-bit into the background over the past four years; taking an increasingly more limited role. In fact last November it had appeared that the aforementioned Ms. Phelps was really serving as de facto assistant.

Fortunately the Chesterbrook and Cooper precincts were close together, with about a ten minute drive separating them. Milton decided that he would visit Chesterbrook at 5:00 a.m., keeping his promise to Cindy, but not stay very long. He would then hightail it over to Cooper and do whatever was needed to get Julia going. After those two precincts, the rest of the day should fall into place.

17(b)

MONDAY EVENING

E<small>VEN AS</small> M<small>ILTON</small> was planning his route Julia Hopkins was preparing to go to bed. A widow in her late eighties, Julia prided herself on her independence and ability to live unassisted. In reality, neighbors had started taking an increasingly active role making sure she was all right and ensuring that her modest house continued to get the maintenance it needed.

Her move from chief to assistant chief four years ago meant that fewer tasks and decisions were now her direct responsibility. Gradually she had allowed younger officers to do more of the things that normally would fall under the purview of the assistant chief.

The truth was that Julia had considered her days as chief election officer to be at an end and had even considered stepping down as assistant and being "just an officer." Then came that phone call from the Government Center. They needed a chief for January 6. Would she do it? Well if they really need me, I guess I can do it one more time, she said. Would there be some good people on her team? Oh yes, nothing but the best she had been assured.

17(c)

MONDAY EVENING

No MATTER HOW many times he did this, Carl always was a bundle of nerves the evening before an election. Once 5:00 a.m. arrived and he could swing into action he was fine, but the night before was always rough. Each election he would set the alarm for 3:30 a.m.; hit the sheets at 9:00 p.m.; and just lie there. Sleep came in a few fits and bursts but mostly it did not come at all.

This time was the added complication that Carl was not the master of his own ship. Somehow he would have to guide and mentor a chief who quite frankly did not seem to want to be either guided or mentored. Carl was genuinely sorry that he and Cindy had got off to such a rough start. She was obviously intelligent and could be quite personable when she wanted to be. She was also rather attractive which he found to be a bit distracting. However her attention to detail, or lack thereof, was maddening and Carl did not look forward to a day of trying to either anticipate her mistakes (ideally) or cleaning up after them.

Complicating the situation was Carl's realization that not all of her ideas were bad. For the five years that he had run the precinct, voters had exited the gym by the same door that they entered.

Occasionally the people travelling in different directions had bumped into each other but Carl had always accepted it as just the way it was. The fact that Cindy had seen a "better way" (and he had to admit that it was a better way) by having voters exit using the side door, after giving it at most a minute or two of thought was rather unsettling.

Carl started to thumb through the manual one more time. Then he stopped. This was ridiculous. Reading the manual again wasn't going to help. He knew the manual. What he needed was a good night's sleep and a willingness to temper his encyclopedic knowledge of the rules with a bit of flexibility to handle the challenges that awaited him. Flexibility. That was one trait he wasn't sure he had.

"I'll guess I'll find out tomorrow," he said as he turned out the bedroom light.

17(d)

MONDAY EVENING

C INDY HAD TO admit it. She was on edge. This was a new experience for her. As one of the rising stars of her marketing firm she was used to making high stakes presentations where her charm and ability to grasp the essentials of the situation usually won the day.

This is what made the election stuff so annoying. None of it was complex. It was simply a matter of following the manual in a cookbook like way. This should be a snap. And it had been a snap last November when she had stepped unofficially into the assistant chief's role and had literally shone. They had all raved about her. Admittedly the chief had given her very specific instructions so no real planning had been involved. And of course some of those aging lions had been a bit smitten by her youthful charm. Yes it had been a rather enjoyable experience, enjoyable enough for her to say without much deliberation, "Sure, I'll serve as chief in January."

Now thanks mainly to Carl, she had become painfully aware of all that she did not know. Since returning to her apartment from the school, she had immersed herself in the manual. While she hardly had it memorized, she now felt that she had a reasonable grasp on where the various topics were.

Deep down she realized that she was probably going to have to rely on Carl quite heavily tomorrow. This bothered her on a number of fronts. By temperament Cindy always wanted to be the one in control. This coupled with Carl's tendency to be preachy and judgmental promised to make tomorrow a very long day.

Well I accepted the gig, Cindy sighed and I need to make it work. She was not particularly idealistic and things like voting and democracy did not especially energize her, although she did realize in some sort of academic sense that they were "important." What she did possess however was a core belief, instilled in her at an early age by her parents, that once undertaken a job should be done well.

Cindy acknowledged that her performance thus far had left something to be desired. Some of her thoughts and words at the school that day had boarded on being petty and she knew that a certain attitude adjustment was in order. She would just have to swallow her pride and work as best she could with Carl.

I just hope he doesn't piss me off completely, she thought, *because if he does, all bets are off and there will be hell to pay.*

18

Tuesday morning, January 6, 4:30 a.m.

MILTON WAS JUST completing his early breakfast when his cell phone rang. He reached for it with trepidation. Cell phone calls at 4:30 a.m. were never good.

"Milton Ayres"

"Milton this is Rosemary Ramirez, your chief over at Hagerman. I'm afraid we have a situation. I need to go to the emergency room."

"Oh no!"

"This has happened before. I don't think it's serious but I do need to go to the ER. The school is on the way and I can drop off my election materials in the parking lot as I pass by."

"Shouldn't you be dialing 911 for an ambulance?"

"No. I'll drive myself. Like I said, this has happened before. Can you be at the school in fifteen minutes?"

Milton assured her that he could and they completed the call. He gathered up his last few things and went out to his car. He was glad he had packed it the night before.

"Every year," he sighed, "I study the particulars of an election and the anticipated challenges of each of the precincts and then I plan out my route. And every year the plan is shot to hell in the first few hours. This however is a new record."

Milton said a silent prayer for Rosemary as he started his car. They had worked together for a number of years and he had grown rather fond of her and her upbeat, positive approach to things.

On a purely practical level, this was the worst thing that could have happened. Milton had intended to focus the first hour or so on the Chesterbrook and Cooper precincts, located in the northern end of the district. That would of course be superseded by the Hagerman emergency.

Milton suspected that Hagerman's assistant chief, one Benjamin Laskey, would need a fair amount of assistance, hand holding, and encouragement as he came to grips with his battlefield promotion. At the very least, Milton would have to stay at Hagerman until he was certain that it would open on time and that everyone was reasonably comfortable with their duties. The fact that Hagerman was located at the southern end of the district dictated that for the first hour or so, Chesterbrook and Cooper would be on their own.

Milton turned on his radio and transmitted his first communication of the day.

"Base, this is Rover 5. I'm heading over to Hagerman for the opening."

Milton was tempted to add "Please call me on my cell" but held back. Getting to Hagerman ASAP was of the essence. He could brief the Command Center on Hagerman's situation later.

"Copy that, Rover 5. Good morning and smooth travels," sounded the voice of Roger Dellman, the county's "Machine Coordinator" who supervised the rovers.

Each precinct in the county had an assigned rover. There were eighteen rovers in the county, each with an assigned number (Rover 1, Rover 2, etc.). "Rover 5" was Milton's Election Day handle. Today, however with only eight precincts voting, Milton was the only rover in the field. Still it had been agreed that he would maintain his "Rover 5" identity for the day. Less confusing that way.

It was 4:45 when Milton pulled into the parking lot of the Hagerman Elementary School. A single flood light shone from the top of the school building providing a limited amount of light for the lot. Already a few cars were parked in the far end, away from the building. All election officers were instructed to do this in order to leave the spaces closer to the school for the voters. Milton parked his car and proceeded to the school door. There were about six or seven people standing by the door but he did not see Rosemary.

"Good Morning," said Milton, trying to sound as cheerful and matter-of-fact as possible. "I'm Milton Ayres, your rover for the day. Is one of you Benjamin Laskey?"

"I am," sounded a high pitched voice.

"Excellent," replied Milton. "Benjamin, can you walk with me for a few minutes? We need to discuss a few things."

After a moment of hesitation Benjamin, looking a bit nervous, came forward, clutching his manual in one hand and a small cooler in the other. His manner and facial expression suggested that he really did not want to take a walk with Milton.

"Benjamin," began Milton. "We have a bit of a situation—ah, here she is now."

A car had just pulled into the parking lot. Milton trotted over to where it had stopped. He wanted to make this transfer as quickly as possible so Rosemary could get on her way to the emergency room.

"My manual and kit are in the backseat," Rosemary called out of the car's front window. "Milton, I'm really sorry to do this to you. You may have to guide Benjamin through the opening."

She then added in a whisper, "I think he's a bit shaky."

Milton opened the back door of the car and quickly took possession of the manual and kit. He closed the door; assured Rosemary that all would be taken care of; and wishing her well, sent her on her way.

He then turned to Benjamin, who as his wide eyed expression suggested, was beginning to comprehend the situation. It was time to come clean.

"Rosemary has had a medical emergency," spoke Milton, directly to Benjamin, but loud enough for the others to hear. "We don't think it's serious but she won't be able to serve today. Benjamin, you will serve as chief election officer. I will stay with you as long as necessary during the opening."

"The Office of Elections said that being an assistant chief would be a snap," said Benjamin whose face had turned ashen. "They said that there wasn't that much involved and it would be a good opportunity to learn the process."

Yeah, they do say that, thought Milton.

"And learn you shall, my friend," said Milton cheerfully. And then to everyone, "Come on folks. Let's go inside and get this sucker on the road."

Once inside the gym, Milton breathed a bit easier. Rosemary and Benjamin had done a really nice job of setting things up the day before. With Milton's help, Benjamin located the oath of office sheet from inside the kit and swore in the team. Then, with Milton whispering in his ear, Benjamin formed his team into various subgroups to attend to the necessary set-up tasks: getting the EPBs primed; powering up the scanner and printing the zero report;

turning on the "Create Ballot" machine for the handicapped vot-ers; counting out the first pack of ballots and putting them into privacy folders; putting up the required signs and posters.

Two partisan poll watchers from the political parties came on the scene and seemed satisfied as they monitored the progress. Gradually as things fell into place, Benjamin began to exude a bit more confidence.

I think we're going to be OK, thought Milton.

That was when his cell phone began to ring.

19

TUESDAY, 4:50 A.M.

"**D**RESS IN LAYERS," they had said. Slacks, button down blouse, jacket, sensible shoes. And at the last minute her winter coat although she was not sure she really needed it. It was unusually mild for January. Temperature in the high 40s. Still there was a chance of precipitation later in the day and it could get colder. You never knew. OK, maybe a sweater too. Plus at the last minute she threw her boots into the mix. A cooler with her lunch and snacks. And of course the almighty kit along with the manual.

And so it was that Cindy pulled into the parking lot at the Chesterbrook Elementary School in her "fully loaded" car. She pulled into a space at the far end of the lot where three other cars were already parked. Turning off the engine she sat for a moment to compose herself.

"OK, let's do it," she said softly.

She then pulled from her car the kit, manual, her handbag, and cooler. The rest of her personal things she would get later. Approaching the school she saw four individuals silhouetted against the door. There was Carl talking to a man and woman with another older man standing a little bit removed.

"Our leader has arrived," said Carl with a flourish.

"Good morning, Carl," said Cindy.

Carl, apparently determined to be the M.C., introduced Cindy to Pam and Jerry Blevens as well as Theodore McDougald. Pam and Jerry both appeared to be in their sixties with Theodore considerably older. They all seemed friendly and Cindy shook hands with each. Millicent LaGrande had not yet arrived.

"The door to the school is still locked," Carl explained. "We're a few minutes early. Tess usually opens things on the dot."

Cindy then pulled out a tape measure from her jacket.

"Since we have an extra minute, I'd like to measure forty feet from the front door down that walkway," she said pointing to the walkway that led down to the sidewalk that ran parallel to the street. Volunteers from the political parties, known as "poll workers," frequently worked on Election Day handing out candidate propaganda as well as "sample ballots" which displayed the "right way" a ballot should be filled in (as per that party). It was all perfectly legal so long as it was done at least forty feet from the door of the polling place.

She went to the door and knelt down and started to pull out the tape. However before she could get far, Carl chimed in.

"That's really not necessary, Cindy. It was measured years ago. That second tree over there is the forty foot mark. It's well known by the poll workers from both parties and it's never been a problem," he said cheerfully.

"Very good. Excellent," said Cindy with a (forced) smile, getting to her feet and putting the tape measure back in her pocket.

Cindy was determined to keep everything cordial and on an even keel but she couldn't help thinking, *how come every time you remember a detail it's a big deal and every time I remember one it's nothing?*

Just then the hall light inside the school came on and shined through the windows that were built into the door.

"It's time," said Carl, his voice brimming with anticipation. He pulled down the latch and opened the door. They all proceeded through the door into the school. Down the short hallway they walked, turning left into a shorter hallway and into the gym. Tess gave them all a cheerful greeting.

"Good morning, Carl," she beamed. "Good morning, everybody."

Tess was as good as her word. Everything was exactly as it had appeared in Cindy's diagram.

"Thank you, Tess," said Cindy with genuine warmth. "This is perfect."

"Cindy, why don't you give me your cooler," offered Pam. "I can put it over there in the far corner where we usually park our personal things. That way you can get started that much quicker."

"Thanks, Pam," replied Cindy, giving her the cooler. She then took the kit and manual over to the chief's table. Kneeling down, she snapped open the kit's latch, and pulled out the primary bundle of forms and signs which were bound together with a couple of industrial strength rubber bands. She opened her manual to the "Opening Polls" tab.

"Let's see," she said. "First thing is to swear in the officers and have them sign the oath sheet. Now where is that pesky little oath sheet?"

The oath sheet was a form that contained the oath of office that election officers had to swear to as well as spaces for their signatures. Cindy removed the rubber bands and started going through the forms, signs, and posters, looking for the oath sheet. She suddenly became aware of someone standing over her. She looked up and saw a middle aged man dressed in a business suit. She had never seen him before.

"Who are you?" she asked, less than graciously.

"I'm with the Republicans," he said handing her a piece of paper. The paper stated that the man before her was David Brown and he had been authorized by the head of the county Republican Party to observe as a "poll watcher." Cindy immediately understood. "Poll watchers" were party representatives who were allowed to observe the election inside the polling place. Unlike the outside "poll workers" who needed no special permission, "poll watchers" were required to present their authorization to the chief election officer and wear a badge identifying them as such.

"Oh, thank you," said Cindy taking the paper.

"We're just getting started. I have a poll watcher badge for you here somewhere," she added, with a bit of irritation in having to suspend her search for the oath sheet.

"I think I know where it is," proclaimed Carl, swooping down on the bundle of forms. He reached in and produced, as if by magic, a badge that read "Poll Watcher, Republican Party" and handed it to Mr. Brown. For once, Cindy was thankful for Carl's intervention.

Cindy continued her search. The forms all seemed to be lumped together but there did not seem to be an oath sheet. She could hear the Blevens and Theodore chatting amicably on the other side of the gym. Mr. Brown started walking around the gym looking at the set-up. Carl stood by, almost at attention. She went through the forms a third time. No oath sheet. She knelt down and examined the rest of the kit's contents. Nothing in the main compartment even looked like a form. She started to unzip the side pockets.

"It won't be in there," said Carl. "That's for extension cords and stuff."

Cindy went back to the bundle on the table.

"It doesn't seem to be here," she said, trying to mask the sinking feeling she began to experience.

"Nonsense," said Carl. "They always put it with the compensation sheet."

"Well here's the compensation sheet, but no oath sheet."

"Where was it when you first inspected the contents of the kit back in December after the meeting?"

Cindy looked up at Carl. Their eyes locked. The agony on her face said it all.

"Don't tell me you didn't?" asked Carl, his face registering a mixture of astonishment and righteous indignation.

"I didn't think—didn't realize—oh shit," she stammered. She had actually been reading the manual very carefully over the past couple of days but her eyes must have brushed past the line that read "check your supplies in the kit against the supply list."

The two of them stood together in deep thought for a full minute. Finally Cindy spoke. She spoke quickly, reflecting the urgency of the situation, but quietly so no one else would hear.

"Carl, you know the oath by heart, don't you."

"Why would you think that?" he asked.

"Because it's exactly the sort of thing you would memorize," she said.

"Well perhaps I do, but what does that have to—," he started to say, somewhat surprised that Cindy seemed to have developed such an accurate assessment of him.

"Write it down," she said pulling out a blank note pad from the bundle and a pen from her jacket pocket.

"The whole oath. On that paper?"

"Yes. Right now."

"But this is silly. Look Cindy, why don't I just administer the oath orally and then—"

"Please Carl, write it down."

"But that would only—"

"Just write down the goddamn oath!" hissed Cindy, slamming her fist on the table.

The other officers in the gym looked over in startled surprise but said nothing. Carl briefly thought about commenting on the propriety of using "goddamn" and "oath" in the same sentence but thought better of it. He quickly wrote down the oath.

"Thank you so very much," she said, giving Carl a rather icy smile.

"All right. Everyone gather round," called out Cindy, regaining some of her poise. "We are going to administer the swearing in. You will raise your right hand and repeat after me. At that point you will be officially sworn in. The actual oath sheet has not arrived yet so you will be signing this sheet of paper. And remember once you take the oath orally, you are sworn in, signature or no."

She was about to start the swearing in, when a load voice interrupted.

"Here I am everyone. Sorry I'm late. Five O Clock. Such an ungodly hour. What a bear! Oh well it can't be helped, I suppose. Look I have brownies for everyone! Let's get started!"

"And you are…?" asked Cindy staring at the lady who had just entered the room. She was a rather large woman who appeared to be in her fifties. She was wearing a fur coat and was holding a tin container, presumably the brownies, triumphantly into the air.

"Oh how silly of me. I am Millicent LaGrande, election officer extraordinaire. Actually I've never done it in my life but it does sound like oodles of fun, doesn't it?"

"Welcome to our team," said Cindy, as briskly as she could, realizing that time was slipping away and the 6:00 a.m. opening loomed. "Please step this way as I am about to administer the oath."

Satisfied that she had made her presence known, Millicent joined the others gathered around Cindy who (finally) administered the oath.

"I do solemnly swear (or affirm) that I will perform the duties for this election according to law and the best of my ability and that I will studiously endeavor to prevent fraud, deceit, and abuse in conducting this election."

She looked down at her cell phone which indicated 5:20 a.m. It had taken twenty minutes just to swear them all in.

"I think you need to get it into gear," said a quiet voice. She looked up and saw Carl looking at her intently. His expression of disapproval said it all.

20

TUESDAY, 5:20 A.M.

O F ALL THE Election Day imperatives that had been thrown at Cindy in training, the one that had been stressed the most was the need to have the polls open at 6:00 a.m. Even the slightest deviation was unacceptable. Hence Cindy fully realized that Carl was right. They needed to get it into gear. But Cindy had a need too, and that was to get Carl out of her sight at least for a little while.

"OK, everyone. Time to get started," she called out.

"Let's see. Theodore, I understand you're experienced at putting up the signs and posters. You can do that. And Carl, why don't you help Theodore with the signs. Pam, you and I can start getting the EPBs going while Jerry and Millicent, you can get the scanner up and verify the zero report. Once those things are done, we'll take it from there. Let me get the cart open so we can start."

Cindy walked briskly over to the precinct cart which was in the corner where Tess had put it. She knelt down and cut the seal, unlocked the cart, and opened its door. She rose to her feet. Carl had followed her.

"What are you trying to prove?" he demanded.

"Whatever can you mean?" she replied, with an air of mock innocence.

Carl's first instinct was to lash out verbally but he held back. That would solve nothing. He needed to choose his words carefully. "Look Cindy," he said. "You are the chief, and I will perform any duty you assign to me. But we have less than forty minutes till opening. So you really need to ask yourself if helping Theodore with the signs is the best way to use me."

They stood there for a moment, staring at each other. Carl broke the silence.

"OK, let me get that canvas bag out of the cart. That's where many of the signs that are not in the kit are located."

He knelt down and pulled out the canvas bag.

"It's a heavy, son of a gun," he said carrying it over to one of the tables. Heaving it onto the table, he pulled down the zipper and began to unload the signs.

"No, wait," called Cindy. Carl looked up at her. He could tell from her expression that she was having a hard time saying the words they both knew needed to be said.

Finally, staring at the floor she said "You work with Pam getting the EPBs ready. I'll find someone else to help Theodore."

"You got it," said Carl triumphantly. He went back to the cart and pulled out the two EPB laptops. "Come on Pam; we've got to fire up these critters."

And so it began. Theodore took the first group of signs and headed to the hallway. Jerry and Millicent went over to the scanner to get things started while Carl and Pam hovered over the EPBs at the check-in table.

And Cindy was left to contemplate how many different ways she could ruin the election.

I can't believe I signed up for this, she thought miserably.

21(a)

TUESDAY, 5:25 A.M.

IT WAS NOT in Cindy's nature to brood long over her mistakes and misfortunes. With the team all working on their initial assignments, she turned to her manual to see what other tasks needed to be attended to. The next item was the "Create Ballot" machine that had to be turned on.

The "Create Ballot" machine was a new purchase by the Office of Elections. It was a touch screen ballot creation device that allowed a voter to mark his/her selections by touching the desired candidate's name on the screen. The session was initiated by an election officer inserting a blank card into the machine. After the choices were confirmed the machine would return the card with the selections made. That card would then be fed into the scanner which would recognize it as a completed ballot.

Handicapped voters who were unable to mark the regular pre-printed ballots due to visual problems or other disabilities had a couple of options. They could designate an assistant to help them fill out their ballot or choose to use the "Create Ballot" machine to produce the ballot for them. "Create Ballot" also came equipped with an audio feature which would allow a person who was totally blind to mark the ballot with the aid of earphones and a keypad that were both plugged into the machine.

The cart contained two of these "Create Ballot" machines but the manual specified using only one. The other would serve as backup. Most handicapped voters actually preferred having someone assist them with the regular preprinted ballots so in reality, the "Create Ballot" machine was rarely used. Cindy recalled it only being used a couple of times the previous November.

She removed one of the machines from the cart and placed it on the table that had been designated for it. She then inserted one end of the power supply into the back of the machine. The other side of the power supply was attached to a power cord which was attached to a surge protector that went into the wall. Having completed that, she unlocked the side panel of the machine and flipped the switch to "on."

A number of messages came onto the screen indicating that the machine was waking up. Suddenly the screen went blank. After a few seconds a single line appeared on the screen:

"Test Fail; Error code 7b3df777102"

Cindy gazed at the error screen for a few moments. "OK," she said softly. "Why don't we just put you back in the cart? Perhaps you can take me with you."

Cindy packed up the malfunctioning machine, returned it to the cart, and pulled out the backup. She put the backup on the table and went through the opening process again. This time everything worked. She was eventually prompted to enter a security code, which she had on a card that had been in the kit. She entered it and after a few more messages, the machine announced it was ready for voters.

The eventual "success" with the "Create Ballot" machine enabled Cindy to feel like she had gained a modicum of control. She took a moment to organize some of the forms and envelopes on the chief's table and then accepted the authorization paper from a Democratic Party poll watcher who had just entered the gym.

It was at that point that she heard Jerry, who was over by the scanner shout, "We need the password Cindy."

21(b)

TUESDAY, 5:25 A.M.

JERRY AND MILLICENT went over to the scanner which stood astride a large black bin with a (locked) door in the front.

"The ballots are fed into the scanner," Jerry explained. "The computer in the scanner takes a photographic image of the ballot. The ballot then drops into a blue plastic bin which is located inside this outer bin. At the end of the day, the printer over here, prints the final results. Then the blue bin containing the ballots is removed and the chief brings it to the Government Center. Then if the results are close or contested, the ballots can always be rescanned or if necessary even counted by hand."

"Marvelous," exclaimed Millicent. "What do we do first?"

"We start by opening this auxiliary bin," said Jerry opening a small door on the side with the key that Cindy had given him. "This is where we insert ballots that for some reason can't be scanned. It's rare for that to happen but if it does, they can be hand counted after the polls close."

Jerry shined his small flashlight into the auxiliary bin.

"It's empty," he said. "Now you have a look."

"Why?"

"Because we are of different political parties and we need to both agree that there are no ballots in the bin. I'm a "D" while you're an "R." This way we can check on each other."

"But you seem like a nice, honest man to me."

Jerry smiled. "Humor me. Just look."

"If you insist," replied Millicent. She leaned over. "Oh yes. Very empty."

Next Jerry knelt down and unlocked the front door of the outer bin, opened it, and pulled out the blue plastic bin. Interlacing plastic flaps covered the bin. Jerry lifted the flaps and peered inside.

"This is where the ballots actually land," he said staring down into the bin. "Looks empty."

"Oh yes, very," said Millicent who seemed to be losing her focus.

"Now I look into the outer black bin itself to make sure no ballots are on its floor or caught up in the mechanism or whatever," said Jerry. He was on his knees with his head literally inside the bin. Here was where Millicent drew the line.

"I am not crawling on my hands and knees through the catacombs of that machine and I am now prepared to declare formally that to my satisfaction there are no spare ballots in the machine, on the machine, under the machine, or in any other nook and cranny that may occur to your fertile imagination."

Jerry got to his feet with a big smile on his face. "Actually, I've done checking."

"Good boy."

"Next, we put the blue plastic bin back in the cart, like so," Jerry said as he slid the bin back inside the outer bin. "And we make sure to raise the flaps once it is inside."

"Whatever for. It would be so much easier just to leave them be."

"Because if we don't, the scanned ballots will land on top of the bin rather than go into it."

"Is that bad? Why should we care where they land?"

"It's OK for a little while but soon the ballots will pile up on the flaps. Eventually they will interfere with the ballots being scanned and the scanner will start rejecting ballots all together."

Jerry then closed and locked the front door of the outer bin.

"Now we get down to business," he said, cutting open the seal on the scanner's lid with his wire cutters.

"This goes to the chief," he added, taking it over to the chef's table. Looking down at the Statement of Results form that Cindy had placed on the table, Jerry could tell that the seal numbers matched. He returned to the scanner, satisfied.

Jerry then unlocked and lifted the lid. Underneath was yet another lid.

"Fascinating," said Millicent. "Is this like one of those Russian nesting dolls?"

"Not really," replied Jerry who was beginning to think that a little bit of Millicent might go a long way. "Now we go to the back of the machine and power it up."

With that Jerry went to the back and with his key unlocked a compartment. Opening the compartment he pulled out a power cord. He examined it for a moment and then went over to the precinct cart, returning in a moment with an extension cord and surge protector. A few quick movements and the scanner was plugged into the outlet.

"Now is when the fun begins," said Jerry. "Watch and be amazed."

With that he unlocked and lifted the inner lid. The underside of the lid was a computer screen. Once it reached a vertical position, it came alive. All kinds of messages started flashing, assuring the user that the machine was doing well and success was only a few moments away. Eventually a giant keyboard appeared prompting the user to type in the password.

"We need the password Cindy," Jerry shouted.

Cindy walked quickly, almost but not quite at a trot, over to the scanner holding the card that contained the various passwords to be used.

"Let's see," she began. "OK here it is, 'SpecialJan6.'"

Jerry keyed in the password and the screen generated some more reassuring messages. Suddenly the sound of their printer could be heard and thermal printer paper could be seen rising out of a slot on the left portion of the scanner. It printed for a while and then stopped.

"This is the so called 'zero report,'" said Jerry. "We need to verify that each of the candidates has zero votes."

All three of them examined the report. It contained some measurements concerning computer memory and the like. Buried among those numbers it proclaimed,

"Total Votes cast 0; Haley – R 0; Weston – D 0; write-in 0."

"Looks good," said Jerry. "Millicent, this is where you and I sign."

"Oh, yes," said Millicent. "This is exciting."

Jerry and Millicent signed the report.

"What are those numbers on the screen?" asked Millicent.

"Those are the protective and public counters," said Jerry. "The protective counter is the number of people who have voted in the history of the machine, sort of like the odometer of the car. The public counter is the number of people who have voted in this election."

"Which now reads zero," said Millicent.

"Exactly," said Jerry. "This just confirms what the zero report has already told us. No one has voted yet. This machine is now ready for the first voter. I now turn this report over our leader and await her further direction."

Jerry handed the zero report to Cindy with a smile and a slight bow. Cindy had watched with interest while Jerry had been explaining things to Millicent. While she pretty much knew it already, it was nice to hear it explained again. She couldn't help but compare Jerry's delivery with Carl's.

With the scanner ready, it was time to move on.

Cindy first tasked Millicent, "I'd like you to find Theodore and help him with the signs. He should be outside."

"Very well," said Millicent with a flourish. "I'm off to the great outdoors in search of Theodore." And with that Millicent marched out of the gym.

Cindy then turned to Jerry,

"I'd like you to break open the box that contains the ballots. There should be six packs of one hundred ballots each. Count to make sure that there are six. Then break open one pack. The other packs go back in the box which is placed back in the locked cart. Count to make sure there are exactly one hundred ballots in the pack. Report to me if there are any variances. Then insert one ballot into each of the manila privacy folders. You'll be at the ballot table handing the ballots to the voters as they appear. When you run low, open another pack, informing me when you do. The ballots and the ballot table will be your primary responsibility today, although I will rotate you a bit later."

Jerry concurred and went off to the cart to get the box.

Cindy returned to the chief's table and inserted the zero report into the appropriate envelope. She was pondering what to do next when she heard Carl's voice.

"Cindy," he called. "We need you over here. We have a bit of a situation."

21(c)

TUESDAY, 5:25 A.M.

THEODORE ENJOYED PUTTING up the signs. It had been his primary set-up responsibility ever since he started working under Carl a number of years ago. Sometimes Carl assigned an inexperienced election officer to work with him but most of the time he did it by himself. This was his domain and he took pride in doing it well.

The first thing Theodore always did was put out the so called "real estate" signs. Each precinct was granted six of those. Each one consisted of a wire frame and a shiny plastic "sleeve" which would contain in big letters such things as "Polling Place" and "Voter Parking Here." Helpful arrows also appeared on some of the signs.

Theodore began by going out to the sidewalk area in front of the entrance to the parking lot. There he planted his two "Polling Place" signs in such a way as to almost invite the passing cars into the lot.

Next came the issue of "voting parking." School would be in session that day. Teachers would park their cars; parents would park their cars; volunteers would park their cars. If election officers did not claim the necessary parking spaces for voters early, they would be snatched up by the non-voting public. Theodore had never actually seen that happen but Carl had told him stories about precincts that had failed to claim their parking spaces and the hardships that had been imposed on the voters as a result.

Carl had been the only chief that Theodore had ever served under and having a new person in charge was a new experience for him. It was early but he sensed a certain amount of tension between Carl and Cindy. He hoped this wasn't the case. Theodore was rather fond of Carl who had mentored him and always showed him respect.

Well, regardless, I have these signs to put up, he thought returning his focus to the problem at hand.

Usually the schools were required to provide ten voter parking places for the November elections. For primaries and special elections like this one, the number was reduced to five. Theodore had two "Voter Parking" real estate signs with pointing arrows. He carefully placed each one into the dirt at the top of a parking space so that the two arrows were pointing inward at each other. The signs were placed seven parking spaces apart. Theodore always liked to "sneak in" an extra parking place or two.

"Hello there! Mr. Theodore!" came the cry from the front door of the school. Millicent came striding down the walkway.

"I'm here to help," she said, her arms outstretched in an expansive gesture.

Theodore thought carefully and then spoke. "All right, there are two signs that are back in the gym that need to be posted on the outside door that the voters will enter by. One says "Vote Here." The other says "Prohibited Activities." It lists all the things that people are not allowed to do in the polling place. I believe they are in the blue canvas bag which I last saw on one of the tables. You need to fasten them to the door with the blue painter's tape. Do you think you can do that?"

"Absolutely. I'll have it done posthaste."

Millicent went off while Theodore attended to his last parking lot task which was to place the "Handicapped Voter Parking" real estate sign in the dirt at the top of the parking space closest to the school. Satisfied with the state of the parking lot he walked up the walkway to the school. About halfway up he planted his final real estate sign which read "Vote Here; Votar Aqui." He then proceeded to the front entrance where Millicent was in the process of putting up the two signs.

"Make sure they're straight. That's right. Very nice," he commented.

"They are lovely, aren't they," said Millicent, admiring her handiwork. "Oh which reminds me. I need to get something."

Millicent turned and went down the walkway toward the parking lot, presumably to get something out of her car.

Theodore chuckled. What was that expression, "suck up all the oxygen in the room?" Still, Theodore had learned a long time ago not to be judgmental.

There was still a lot for Theodore to do. He went back into the school and with the blue painters tape attached a number of arrows on the walls to help guide people to the gym. He then entered the gym to gather up all those signs that needed to be posted inside the building. Many of these signs were required to be in the gym itself.

There were posters for all sorts of things: how to mark your ballot; photo ID required; voter rights and responsibilities; a sample ballot for this election; and last but not least, a colorful detailed map of the county with the boundaries of all the precincts.

Having done all those things, Theodore allowed himself to relax for a moment and gaze around the gym. As far as he could tell, everything looked great. Then he looked over to the EPB check-in table and that's when he noticed that Cindy, Carl, and Pam were hovering over one of the EPBs. They did not look happy.

22

TUESDAY, 5:38 A.M.

"**C**INDY," CARL CALLED. "We need you over here. We have a bit of a situation."

Cindy walked/trotted over to the Electronic Pollbook table as quickly as she could. It was these EPBs that contained all the names, addresses, and other vitals for the voters in the precinct. They needed the EPBs to check in the voters. Any "situation" involving EPBs was not a good thing.

"One EPB came up fine," said Carl, pointing to the laptop that Pam was sitting next to. "But this one is on some sort of 'read only mode.' We can't get it to complete the opening sequence."

"What have you tried?" asked Cindy.

"Not a whole lot," Carl replied. "We tried rebooting it once but the same thing came up. The instructions are very specific and don't mention any workaround."

I'm amazed, thought Cindy. *There's actually something you don't know.*

Cindy pulled out her cell phone, "I'm calling Milton."

Milton answered on the second ring.

"Milton we have a problem. One of the EPBs won't come up. Something about a read-only file."

There was a pause of a few seconds. Then Milton responded. "I think I know what the problem is and I have a fix for it. I'm at Hagerman right now. I'll get on the road right away but it will take me fifteen minutes or so to get to you. You probably will have to open with a single EPB. But don't worry. Once I get the other one fixed they will sync together."

"OK, Milton. We'll see you when you get here."

Cindy explained the situation to Pam and Carl. She then looked around at the gym. Jerry was putting ballots into privacy folders. Apparently the first pack had added up to one hundred. Theodore was standing to one side; apparently he and Millicent had put up all the signs.

Cindy suddenly realized; the privacy booths! They needed to place the three sided cardboard privacy booths on the table that the voters would use to mark their ballot. She turned back to Carl, but he wasn't there. Looking across the room she saw him kneeling down in front of the cart pulling out the privacy booths. He then took them over to the table and started setting them up. He then quickly returned to the canvas bag and pulled out a bundle of pens which he took over to the booths placing a pen in each.

She looked at Pam who had settled in, in front of the one functioning EPB. "Does he always know exactly what to do?" she asked gesturing toward Carl.

"Pretty amazing, isn't it," said Pam. "I've worked for a lot of chiefs over the years but he is a one of a kind."

She looked at her cell phone. 5:42 a.m. "Well we just need to wait for Milton," she said to Pam. "So why don't I call the team together and give the opening assignments."

She then proceeded to call the team to gather round and they all met by the chief's table.

"Thank you all for getting everything set up so quickly. We will be opening with only one EPB but the rover is on the way so that should get resolved pretty soon. We will start off with Pam and Carl at the EPB table; Jerry you're at the ballot table; Theodore, you will be at the scanner; I'll be floating around, filling in when necessary; Millicent you can start as greeter. Wait—where is Millicent?"

People looked at each other. No one had an answer.

"Theodore, she was out with you, wasn't she?"

"Yes, but she said that she had to get something...I think... from her car...I think."

"Well she will be the greeter when she gets back inside."

Cindy then read some of the emergency and safety procedures that she was required to go over. It was fairly dry stuff but they all listened politely, if not intently. She then got out the two way radio that she had been issued and turned it on. She would be using it at 6:00 a.m. to inform the Command Center that the polls were open. Right now only a little bit of static was coming from the radio but in a few minutes the airwaves would be full of opening announcements from the eight precincts.

She was also aware that on the dot of 6:00 a.m. she would be required to go out to the front of the school and announce, as the town criers of old used to do, "The polls are now open."

Cindy glanced down at her cell phone. It was 5:49 a.m. Where was Milton? And where was Millicent?

23

TUESDAY, 5:52 A.M.

MILTON STRODE ACROSS the parking lot toward the Chesterbrook Elementary School. He carried with him his manual and, just in case, an extra EPB. He probably wouldn't need it though. As Cindy had explained it, the problem seemed simple enough.

Milton enjoyed his job. His technical skill and easy going manner made him very popular among the chiefs. It was satisfying work; to be greeted at the door by a frenzied chief and then being able to figure out what the problem was and make it right. Helping Benjamin get his footing over at Hagerman had been especially gratifying.

Milton entered the school, proceeded to the gym, and walked over to the table where the EPBs were. He recognized Carl Marsden, of course. He guessed that the younger of the two women was Cynthia Phelps. He remembered her from Cooper the previous November as well as from the chiefs meeting back in December.

"Hi, I'm Milton. Would you be Cynthia Phelps?"

"Yes, I'm Cindy. And here is our delinquent machine," said Cindy, pointing at the malfunctioning laptop.

Milton took a seat in front of the EPB.

"Yes, exactly as I thought," he said. "This machine still has last November's election on it. See where it says 'voters 957'? I'll get this file removed right away. Of course then I'll have to reboot and bring up the normal sequence so it will be about ten minutes before we can get this EPB operational. So you will be opening with just the one."

Milton removed the Chesterbrook specific flash drive from the EPB and replaced it with one that he had taken from his pocket. Immediately a window appeared on the screen. Milton hit a couple of keys and a message appeared that said "election deleted." Then he clicked on the appropriate icons to power down the machine. When the screen went black, Milton switched the flash drives putting the Chesterbrook flash drive back in the laptop. He then pushed the power button.

"OK, moving forward, we're talking ten minutes. But then it will sync with your other EPB and you'll be back to being fully operational."

"Thank you, Milton," said Cindy. "You're a life saver."

Looking at her cell she saw that it was 5:58 a.m. Two minutes to go. Raising her head she saw a line of would-be voters edging into the gym.

"We're not open yet," she called. "Two more minutes."

Cindy then pondered which of her two opening tasks to do first. "Do I go out to the front of the school and make the opening announcement first or do I radio in to the Command Center that we are open? I suppose I should make the announcement first, and then get back in as soon—"

"Cindy," said Pam who had been sitting in front of the other (good) EPB. There was a note of concern in her voice. "I think we may have a problem."

"What!" cried Cindy and Carl in unison.

"The mouse pointer; it won't move," said Pam said, moving the mouse back and forth on the mousepad to make her point.

"The screen's frozen," said Carl. "Try pressing a key. Any key."

Pam pressed a key. Nothing. Another key. Still nothing.

"I think it's six o'clock," called the man at the front of the line.

"Milton, the screen just froze on the good EPB," said Cindy, a sense of panic in her voice. "Can you do something? Anything?"

"It really is six," called the man. "Look, my cell phone says 6:00 a.m.," he said, showing it to the person in line behind him.

"I'll have to either reboot or replace that machine," responded Milton even as he was working on getting the first EPB up and running. "This thing is still five minutes away. You'll have to open with the backup paper pollbook."

Suddenly the two way radio came alive with sound.

"Base, this is the Easthampton precinct. We are open for business and are checking in our first voter now."

"Copy that, Easthampton. Well done. You are the first to report."

"Cindy," said Carl, with urgency in his voice. "We need that paper pollbook right now. It should be in the kit."

Cindy was panic stricken. Kicking off her shoes, she ran as fast as she could across the gym to where the kit was to hunt for the paper pollbook. Sound bombarded her from every direction.

"Did you hear that? They're voting at Easthampton. Why aren't we open yet?"

More static followed by *"Base, the Wallingford precinct is now up and running."*

"Copy that, Wallingford. Well Done."

Cindy started rummaging through the kit looking for the paper pollbook. It had to be in here somewhere. Dear Lord, please.

"Base, this is the Danby precinct. We are open."

"Copy that, Danby. Welcome aboard."

There! She had it. She started back holding the precious paper pollbook.

"Cindy, don't forget the paper pollbook count sheet as well," shouted Carl.

"They're open everywhere. Why aren't they open here? Is something wrong? I need to get to work."

Cindy returned to the kit and began searching for the count sheet. She suspected (hoped) it would be in just about the same place that the pollbook was.

And there it was. Bingo!

"I've got them both," she shouted running back to the EPB table. Over the static, a booming voice could be heard,

"Base, this is Manchester, the biggest and the best precinct in the district. We are open and have a line of twenty-five voters."

"Copy that, Manchester. Modest as always."

"Here Carl," gasped Cindy handing him the paper pollbook and count sheet. "Can we get it open with this?"

"Sure can. Do you want to give the signal?"

Cindy gave a wave. "Come on in, we are open."

"Finally. What took them so long?"

The man who was first in line approached the table.

"Your full name please," asked Carl.

"Thomas Raymond Debinger," said the man. "I can spell if you want."

"That shouldn't be necessary. May I see your ID please?"

Mr. Debinger produced his ID. Carl compared the photo on the ID to the man standing in front of them. They matched.

"Excellent. Let's find you in the pollbook," said Carl, leafing through the paper pollbook, looking for the "D"s. It really was a lot slower than using the EPBs.

"Ah, here you are," said Carl. "And your address please."

"485 Carter Run Court."

Carl then repeated in an audible voice so the two party poll watchers at the side table could hear,

"Thomas Raymond Debinger; 485 Carter Run Court."

"Now Mr. Debinger let me give you...oops, Cindy, where are the ballot cards?"

Oh crap, thought Cindy who was just getting her breath back. "I'm sure they're back in the kit."

"Come on, Cindy. Get in the game!" snapped Carl.

Once again she ran the length of the gym to where the kit was.

"Base, Seneca Grove precinct is open."

"Copy that, Seneca Grove. Glad to hear it."

Looking inside the kit, Cindy located the deck of ballot cards, neatly wrapped with a rubber band. Hoping that this would be her last cross gymnasium sprint, at least for a little while, she allowed herself the luxury of a brisk walk.

"Well I don't see why I need a ballot card," Mr. Debinger was complaining. "Can't you use hand signals or something?"

"Here is your ballot card, Mr. Debinger," said Cindy handing him the card from the top of the pile. "If you step around here to the ballot table, you will receive your ballot."

Mr. Debinger accepted the card and proceeded to the ballot table. Cindy handed the rest of the deck to Carl. She was then aware that someone was behind her. She turned around. It was Theodore.

"I believe these are yours," he said with a smile, holding up her shoes.

"Thank you, Theodore," said Cindy. "Now I can make my curbside announcement with a modicum of dignity."

"You're most welcome," he replied and returned to his station at the scanner.

"Actually," she said, looking at the queue of voters. "I don't see much point at all in making that opening announcement. I think they've figured it out by now."

"It is the law and tradition," said Carl in his somewhat preachy tone. "I can do it for you if you'd like, providing you take my place here."

"No, I'll do it," sighed Cindy. It was obvious that Carl knew what he was doing with the paper books, which she had never used.

Cindy walked past the line of about ten voters and through the door leading to the hallway. As she exited the gym she could hear the sound from the static infested radio.

"We still haven't heard from Hagerman, Chesterbrook, and Cooper. Please call in. We need to confirm that you are open."

Cindy continued to the front door, passing incoming voters on the way. It was still dark. People could be seen getting out of their cars. She noticed that the partisan poll workers had set up separate tables out by the tree, thereby respecting the forty foot rule. Other poll workers were on the walkway leading to the parking lot, handing out literature to the voters as they approached the school. They too appeared to be at least forty feet from the front door.

Feeling a bit silly, she gave a rather halfhearted, "The polls are now open." and went back inside.

Returning to the gym she could tell that the line was growing. Perhaps fifteen voters. Having only one line, and that with a paper pollbook was costing them.

"Hagerman, Chesterbrook, and Cooper. We need to hear from you."

"Cindy," Milton called. "This EPB is now ready. I'm going to start working on the other one now. You need to call the Government Center. Normally when we start using paper pollbooks, we're required to use them for the rest of the day but in this case when so few people have been checked in, they will usually give you a waiver. How many have checked in so far, Carl?"

"Five," said Carl. "I'm on number six."

A high pitched voice came out of the radio. *"Base, this is Hagerman and we are—wait, are we? —yes, we are open and processing voters."*

"Way to go, Benjamin," said Milton quietly.

"Copy that, Hagerman. And thank you. Where are you Chesterbrook and Cooper?"

Picking up the radio, Cindy pressed the transmit button and feigning a calmness she did not feel checked in, *"Base, Chesterbrook is right here; we are open and things couldn't be better."*

Even as Carl rolled his eyes, and the radio came out with a *"Welcome aboard Chesterbrook. We're waiting on you Cooper,"* she was dialing the Government Center.

"Roger Dellman."

"Roger, this is Cindy Phelps over at Chesterbrook."

"You gave us a bit of a scare, Cindy."

"Sorry about that but it's been a scary morning. Both EPBs went belly-up and we had to open with the paper pollbook. Milton has got one of the EPBs going now but he says we need your permission to switch over."

"How many have voted so far?"

"Carl, what's the count?" she called over to him.

"Six. And I'm checking in number seven now," was his response.

"Roger, it's six going on seven."

"OK, make number seven the last one we check in on paper. Have all remaining voters check in with the EPBs. In between each new EPB voter, check in one of the paper pollbook people in the EPB. Repeat until all seven are done. Who do you have working at the check-in table?"

"Carl Marsden is checking them in with the paper pollbook and Pam Blevens is on the EPB."

"Good. They're both solid. You should be fine. And if Milton is still there, could you ask him to head on over to Cooper?"

"Will do. Thanks, Roger. Bye."

Cindy repeated Roger's instructions to Carl and Pam and they both seemed comfortable with the drill. While this had been going on Milton had replaced the other EPB with his own and was now booting it up with the Chesterbrook flash drive inserted. These flash drives were precinct specific containing all the registered voters for the precinct.

"Milton, Roger Dellman wants you to head on over to Cooper when you're done here," said Cindy.

"That should be in about ten minutes, once we get this up and synced," replied Milton.

At that moment the radio sounded. The voice coming out was slow and deliberate. *"Base, the Cooper precinct is open. Repeat. We are open."*

Cindy and Milton exchanged glances.

"Julia came through," said Cindy quietly.

"Apparently," agreed Milton.

"Copy that, Cooper and thanks. All precincts are now confirmed as being open. To all chiefs; to all chiefs. Your next call in will be 10:00 a.m. when you will report your vote totals. Have a great morning everyone."

Cindy got to her feet and looked around. It was the first moment since their 5:00 a.m. start that she had had the opportunity to take stock and even relax for a moment. Pam was checking in the voters on the EPB and things were going quicker now with Carl helping to retrofit those early paper pollbook voters into the system. Milton was well on his way to getting the second EPB operational.

Over at the ballot table, Jerry was collecting the ballot cards and handing out the ballots in the privacy folders. Ideally they should have someone stationed where people marked their ballots in the privacy booths, should questions arise, but the ballot was simple and these early voters knew what they were doing. Perhaps later in the day Cindy would revisit that. At the scanner, Theodore was politely standing to one side as the voters inserted their completed ballot. He would then hand them an "I Voted" sticker and point to the side exit door.

It had been so chaotic, only a few minutes earlier but now things seemed to have magically fallen into place. It wasn't perfect of course. They still could use a greeter to help control the line. That was supposed to be Millicent's job. Cindy gave a short gasp. She had completely forgotten about Millicent during the various crises of the past thirty minutes. But obviously something wasn't right.

Where was Millicent?

24

TUESDAY, 6:20 A.M.

HAVING SUCCESSFULLY PROVIDED Chesterbrook with two functioning EPBs, Milton returned to his car, determined to get over to Cooper as soon as possible. Milton liked what he had seen at Chesterbook. Although inexperienced, Cindy Phelps had seemed bright and tenacious, well able to recover and learn from whatever mistakes she might make. And having seasoned pros like Carl Marsden and Pam Blevens behind her would certainly help. No, Milton was not worried about Chesterbrook.

Cooper was a different story. As he pulled out of the parking lot into main road, Milton was anxious to get over to Cooper and see how Julia Hopkins was doing. It was a short drive to get over there, maybe ten minutes or so.

I'll soon find out, he thought.

Suddenly his cell phone rang.

Milton sighed and pulled over to the side of the road. He picked up his phone.

"Milton Ayres, here."

"Milton, this is Benjamin Laskey over at Hagerman. You need to get back over here right away. It's a disaster. The scanner isn't taking the ballots. It's spitting them out as soon as the voter puts them in. Then it beeps at us. What should I do? What should I do?"

"OK, let's calm down. Is there any message on the screen when it rejects the ballot?"

"None. It just spits the ballot back. And we had the voter try inserting the ballot every which way, you know, face up, face down, top first, bottom first. Nothing works. So then we suggested that the voter filled out the ballot wrong and we gave him a fresh ballot. While he was filling out his new ballot, the next voter tried to insert her ballot. And that rejected too. They're all rejecting. And the scanner keeps beeping at us. It's a nightmare. Please come right away. What should I do?"

"Has this been from the beginning or did it just start happening now?"

"It worked perfectly for the first fifteen minutes but now it's rejecting them. And our line of voters is growing. What should I do? What should I do?"

From Benjamin's description, Milton was pretty sure what the problem was. In his calmest, most soothing voice he began to explain.

"Benjamin, I think I know what the problem is and I can talk you through it but you need to stay calm. Let's see; you're Republican. I want you to select one of your Democratic officers, preferably your most capable."

"That would be Kathy."

"Very good. I want you and Kathy to go over to the metal bin that the scanner rests on, unlock it, and look inside. And invite the party poll watchers to observe you. After you open it tell me what you see."

For the next couple of minutes Milton listened to bits of conversations as Benjamin assembled Kathy and the poll watchers. At last Benjamin reported back,

"We have opened the door."

"And what do you see?"

"Well there's the blue bin with a pile of ballots on top."

"Exactly what I thought. Whoever set up the scanner forgot to open the top flaps of the blue bin. What you need to do is slide the blue bin out, open the flaps and put in all those ballots. Make sure the poll watchers understand what you are doing. Check the inside of the outer metal bin as well in case any ballots slid down the side of the blue bin.

After about fifteen seconds, "OK, we've done that."

"Now slide the blue bin back inside. And this time remember to lift the flaps. After that you can close and lock the outer bin."

A brief pause, then, "Done."

"OK, now have the first voter on line insert his ballot and see what happens."

After a second or two, Milton could hear the sound of cheers coming from the phone.

"It's working! It's working!"

"Well done Benjamin. Let me know if you have any more problems."

"I'll do that. Thanks, Milton."

His mission accomplished, Milton pulled out into the road. He suspected that he would be hearing a lot more from Benjamin as the day progressed.

A few minutes later Milton pulled into the Cooper Middle School parking lot. He frowned at what he saw. Or rather what he didn't see. No election signs at all. No "Polling Place" signs. No "Voter Parking" signs. Nothing. Milton knew that the middle school started its day at a little after 7:00 a.m. This meant teachers and others would soon be arriving and parking their cars. At a very minimum, they needed to get the "voter parking" signs up as quickly as possible. Otherwise the voters would have a tough time finding suitable parking.

Milton got out of his car and proceeded to the school entrance. There were party poll workers outside the building handing out their propaganda but no polling place signs. Once inside the building he did see a couple of adults holding what looked like party fliers enter a room about half way down the hall. As he walked down the hall he was passed by a woman walking in the other direction. Milton noticed the "I Voted" sticker on her coat. It would appear that the Copper precinct was functioning.

Entering the classroom, Milton was relieved to see that the room was set up, more or less in an acceptable fashion. A small line of voters was queued up at the EPB table. To the other side of the room were tables where a couple of voters were marking their ballots and in the corner was the scanner. It wasn't the greatest set-up in the world in terms of efficiency but it was functional.

"Hello, Milton," called Julia Hopkins, sitting by herself beside the ballot marking table. "It was nip and tuck, but we got it open."

"Yes you did, Julia. It looks good in here. But the signage is a bit scarce. Tell me, who is your assistant chief?"

"That would be Nelly," said Julia pointing to a plump, gray haired woman seated by the scanner.

"Excellent," replied Milton. "I wonder if I could borrow Nelly for a few minutes to put up some more signs. Could you relieve her at the scanner for a bit?"

Julia readily agreed and Milton set to work with Nelly getting the signs out of the kit and canvas bag. Milton's initial concern was getting the "Polling Place" and "Voter Parking" signs out into the parking lot and within a few minutes he and Nelly were in possession of the signs and heading down the hall.

"Nelly," Milton said as they walked. "Julia has a world of experience and we are very fortunate that she is still willing to serve as chief. However she does miss some of the details so I need you to keep a close tab on things. As the day progresses have your copy of the manual out and just make sure that everything that should be happening is happening. Can you do that?"

"Oh yes," said Nelly who seemed like a pleasant, cheerful soul. "I'm sure everything will be just lovely."

I hope so, thought Milton. *I really do.*

25

TUESDAY, 6:35 A.M.

ONCE THE INITIAL EPB crisis had passed there was relatively little for Cindy to do. These early voters were "regulars," people on their way to work. They were experienced in how the process operated and went through the check-in and voting procedures quickly. For the most part they were pleasant enough but had no real desire to linger and chat. All they wanted to do was vote as quickly as possible and be on their way. The "special needs" voters would not come until later.

Cindy used this time of respite to organize the forms and envelopes on the chief's table. She also began to seriously ponder the question of what, if anything, to do about her missing election officer. Should she called the Command Center? If Millicent really had flown the coop, then they were down to only five officers. That was fine for now while everything was going smoothly but what if things got hectic later? And what if Millicent had hurt herself? Images of her helplessly floundering in some unknown ditch by the side of the parking lot began to intrude on Cindy's mind.

Then, just about when she had decided to call the Command Center, who should come bursting in through the gym door, almost colliding with a couple of entering voters, than Millicent LaGrande herself.

"Frappuccinos for everybody!" she cried, holding her tray of beverages aloft for all to see. "I'm sorry I'm so late. The line at Starbuck's was absolutely horrid. But it couldn't be helped. How else are we supposed to function at such a ghastly hour? Call out your favorites but I must warn you. The Carmel Light is mine."

Cindy opened her mouth in amazement. What was Millicent thinking? In all of her training it had been emphasized, "When you sign up, it is for the entire day. You may not leave the premises at all. No exceptions." If someone forgot something from their car, it was OK to retrieve it, but that was it.

As Millicent started handing out the beverages, Carl left his post and hurried back to Cindy.

"You have to send her home," he said with severe certainty. "No one is allowed to leave the voting location during the day. That's the rule. If you leave, you're finished."

"Hold on," replied Cindy. "I agree that what she did was incredibly stupid. But do we really have to send her away? After all, no harm was done and we really could use that sixth officer."

"No, she has to go."

"But—"

"You have no choice. Trust me Cindy, I'm not making this stuff up. You have to follow the rules. All the rules, not just the ones you like. That's what you signed up for."

Cindy sighed, "OK, let me call the Command Center."

Quickly, she dialed the Command Center. In the background she could hear Millicent's stream of chatter.

"Roger, we have a bit of an issue here. One of my officers, quite thoughtlessly left the polling place for a Starbuck's run. Carl insists that we have to send her home."

"How long was she gone?"

"Probably about an hour."

"Carl's right. She has to go."

"Come on Roger. Do we have to be so hardass?"

"Cindy, we really don't have any choice on this one."

The silence hung heavy for a moment.

"Roger, this job sucks," said Cindy quietly.

More silence.

"There is one thing I can offer," said Roger. "The county has allowed some people to sign up as a.m. or p.m. officers. It's not done a lot but it is done. You can give her the opportunity to return at Noon to be a p.m. officer. But for now she has to leave."

"Well I guess that's something. I'll see if she'll go for it."

"I'm sorry I can't offer more."

"Me too. Bye Roger."

Feeling absolutely miserable Cindy looked over at Millicent who was drinking her coffee and prattling on to Theodore about her favorite beverages. Knowing that she had no choice, she walked over to where the two of them stood.

"Ah my fearless leader," proclaimed Millicent. "What would thou hath me do now?"

Cindy swallowed hard and began. "Millicent I'm terribly sorry but you have to leave. The rules are that no one can leave the polling place once we have gathered. You left us for an hour without telling anyone of your plans. I wish I could make an exception but my hands are tied. You have to go."

"Oh don't be silly," said Millicent. "Those rules are all well and good but no one follows them exactly. Here, have a Frappuccino. That will put a smile back on your face."

"Millicent, please don't make this harder than it already is. You have to leave."

Gradually as the seconds ticked off, Millicent began to understand the situation. Her larger than life countenance seemed to shrink before Cindy's eyes.

"But I only wanted to help—" she stammered.

"Of course you did," said Cindy. She reached out to touch Millicent, to somehow comfort her, but Millicent suddenly shrank back. A deathly silence engulfed the two of them, made even more pronounced by the background noise of voters being processed.

"Well I guess I should be on my way," she said at last, trying to regain a measure of her old bravado.

"They did say that if you want, you can return at Noon to be a p.m. officer," said Cindy, desperately trying to end the encounter with a note of optimism.

"Noon?" said Millicent. "Well I don't know. I really—No, I don't think so. I have a lot on my plate you know and I really must be going."

With that Millicent turned around and with as much dignity as she could manage left the room.

Cindy just stood there, staring at the wall. In the background she could hear Pam checking in a voter while another voter approached Theodore with his ballot and inserted it into the scanner.

Once again Carl left his EPB station and approached Cindy.

"I know that was tough but you had—"

"Don't say a word," said Cindy. Her raw anger came through as she spoke each word slowly and distinctly.

"But surely you realize—"

"Carl, so help me, if you say another word I'm going to lose it. Because of you, I just publically humiliated that harmless, kindhearted woman. I realize that we are stuck together for the rest of the day. I will speak to you when it is absolutely necessary. You will speak to me when it is absolutely necessary. And when the day is over we will hopefully never lay eyes on each other again. Now go back to your station and don't say another word."

26

Tuesday, 6:50 a.m.

THE WHOLE INCIDENT with Millicent coupled with everything else that had happened that morning, had left Cindy emotionally exhausted. *"I'm not even an hour into the day and already I'm spent,"* she reflected.

She looked around for something to do. This business of "just supervising" was not doing it for her, at least not in her present frame of mind. She needed something concrete. Anything.

For a few minutes she watched Jerry at the ballot table. A voter would come to the table holding the voter card he/she had received at the EPB check-in. Jerry would take the card and give the voter a ballot inside a privacy folder and direct the voter to the table where the ballot would be marked. Every so often he would take his pile of ballot cards back to the EPB table, even as every so often Theodore would bring him the empty folders that were discarded by the voters once they inserted their ballots into the scanner. It was a very orderly, almost mechanical like process.

Cindy approached Jerry. "How are you fixed for ballots?" she asked.

"I'm over half way through the first pack," he said. "My guess is that I've still got thirty or so."

"Why don't I count out the next pack of one hundred for you?"

"That would be great. We'll need them pretty soon, I'm sure."

So for the next ten minutes she worked at the chief's table sorting ballots into piles of ten, making especially certain that none of the ballots were sticking together. At last she was able to confirm that there were indeed one hundred ballots in the pack. She was in the process of turning the ballots over to Jerry when her cell phone rang.

"Cindy, this is Roger again. We've just had word from the Republicans that Jennifer Haley and her entourage are on their way over to your precinct so she can vote. We think the TV crew from the local news station will be there as well. Try to make sure you have your best people process her."

Cindy wanted to say, *"I'm down to five officers, Roger. She's lucky we have anyone here at all,"* but thought better of it.

Rather she replied with, "Thanks for the heads-up, Roger. We'll do everything we can to make sure they feel welcome and that things go smoothly."

"Great. Now I do have to ask. Has your 'problem officer' left the polling place?"

"Yes, she has," replied Cindy coldly.

"Thank you. I just had to ask. Well good luck."

Cindy hung up, looking down at her cell for the time. It was 7:00 a.m. on the dot. Time for a numbers check. Every hour on the hour, if practicable, chiefs were asked to record the number of voters checked in on the EPBs and compare that with the public count on the scanner. They should be the same and chiefs were expected to account for instances when they were not.

Cindy approached Theodore at the scanner who had just given an "I Voted" sticker to his latest voter.

"What's our public count, Theodore?" she asked.

"Let's see," he said, leaning over to read the screen. "Ah yes, we stand at 82."

She looked over to the privacy table and saw three voters working on their ballots. At the EPB table Carl and Pam were each checking in a single voter.

Walking briskly over to the EPB table, Cindy did a quick tabulation in her head. *"82 plus the three working on their ballots plus two checking in. So the EPB count should be 87."*

She deliberately went over to Pam's side of the table. Pam had just finished checking in the voter and had given her a ballot card. Cindy looked at the EPB screen and saw that it said "Voters 86."

She frowned. "I was hoping to see 87."

"You will in a second," Pam assured her. "Carl here, has just checked in a voter. It does take a few seconds for the EPBs to communicate to each other via the cable."

Carl, expressionless, looked straight ahead, apparently determined not to say anything. Cindy continued to stare at the EPB screen. The number changed to 87.

She breathed a bit easier. "Just as advertised. Thank you, Pam."

Returning to the chief's table, Cindy recorded the number in a grid that had been set up in the manual. She then reflected upon what to do concerning the anticipated arrival of the Republican candidate. The staffing was really as good as it could be. The place with the biggest chance for a snafu was the EPB table. That's where you wanted the best and that's what Carl and Pam were. Jerry had the ballot table well in hand. Theodore might look frail but he seemed to be doing OK at the scanner. Cindy made a mental note to give him a break once the pending excitement had passed.

As for herself, Cindy had decided she would serve as greeter and facilitator. She realized that she also needed to alert the team or at least the assistant chief. She walked over to Pam's side of the EPB table.

"Pam," she said, with sufficient volume that Carl couldn't help but hear. "I've been advised that Jennifer Haley will be here to vote, momentarily. She will be treated exactly the same as any other voter and will be checked in by either you or Carl in the normal sequence of things. It will be my job to make sure her presence doesn't disrupt things too much. I'm going out to the front to see if she has arrived yet."

Pam smiled and assured Cindy that they would be ready. Cindy then walked across the gym and into the hallway passing a trickle of incoming voters on the way. Emerging from the front of the building she saw that the first glimmer of dawn was beginning to appear.

But that was only of passing interest for down the front sidewalk, just past the forty foot boundary, an intense spotlight shone on a woman who Cindy immediately recognized from the newspaper photos as Jennifer Haley, the Republican candidate. It appeared that she was holding some sort of news conference. Cindy realized that as she was outside the forty foot line, it was not her place to interfere or even directly observe. Rather she remained in the doorway where she did manage to hear snippets of the candidate's remarks.

"...unlike our opponent we have discussed the issues... very concerned about voter fraud...confident of the outcome..."

At that point the news conference concluded and the candidate appeared to be preparing to come up the walkway to the school. Cindy decided it would be best to greet her at the door of the gym and it was to the gym that she returned.

Entering the gym, she pointed toward Carl and Pam and they both nodded. They were ready.

27

TUESDAY, 7:10 A.M.

THE BRIGHT LIGHT shone in her eyes. It was disorienting, almost blinding. The candidate stepped forward. She was about forty and fashionably dressed with platinum blond hair. She flashed what undoubtedly was her most radiant smile and held out her hand.

"Hi, I'm Jennifer Haley. I'd like to vote please."

Cindy took her hand, returning what she hoped was her best smile. "Hello, I'm Cynthia Phelps, chief election officer. Welcome to the Chesterbrook precinct. If you step this way there are just a couple of people in line in front of you. We will have you voting in a minute."

Cindy led the candidate over to the line and then retreated from the immediate scene. She was the greeter and she had greeted. While she would keep tabs from a distance it was up to the rest of the team to provide the service. Cindy walked back over to the chief's table. When she got there, she realized that she had been followed.

She was a young woman, about Cindy's age. A man holding what appeared to be a camera in one hand and spotlight in another accompanied her.

"Hi, I'm Tracy Miller, WMML local news," she said with a big smile offering her hand.

"Cynthia Phelps," replied Cindy returning her smile, shaking hands and thinking, *I'm sick of smiling like a Cheshire cat.*

"I was wondering if you would consent to a brief interview," asked Tracy.

"So long as it really is brief," said Cindy parroting the "company line" from the manual. "I am busy assisting the voters."

"Of course," said Tracy, her smile seemingly frozen in place. She nodded to the cameraman. Once again Cindy was nearly blinded by the light.

"This is Tracy Miller, speaking to you from the Chesterbrook precinct which promises to be one of the critical battlegrounds in today's special election which will determine which political party will control Virginia's State Senate. We're here with Cynthia Phelps, the chief election officer for Chesterbrook. Cynthia, could you describe the mood here as people are casting their critical votes?"

"Well Tracy, things are very smooth and businesslike here. People are arriving, waiting in line patiently, and voting. The process is working just like it's supposed to."

"Excellent. And from your perspective, how do you read the mood of the voters? Do you sense a Republican or Democratic trend?"

Cindy had all she could do to keep her smile in place. *You little minx*, she thought. *You know I can't answer something like that.*

"We will know the mood of the voters shortly after 7:00 p.m. when the votes are tabulated. Anything prior to that is just idle speculation."

"And speaking of votes. How many people have voted so far?"

"As of 7:00 a.m. we had 87 voters."

"So projected over a thirteen hour day that would mean over a thousand voters. Does Chesterbrook have a sufficient number of ballots to handle that kind of turnout?"

Cindy briefly reflected on the 600 ballots that the precinct had been allocated. Measured against Tracy's instant math that seemed a bit shaky. But this wasn't the time or place to articulate any doubts. Smile in place. Forge ahead.

"Tracy, we are looking forward to a robust turnout and each and every voter will receive a ballot."

She was beginning to feel this interview had gone far enough but Tracy seemed in no mood to quit.

"Excellent answer. Now there have been, in recent elections, allegations of voter fraud. What safeguards has the Chesterbrook precinct put in place to prevent such an occurrence?"

"All of our election officers have been thoroughly trained in the correct procedures according to the law and those procedures are being followed. Now if you'll excuse me, I do have things I need to do."

"Fine. Fine. But I do have just one final question."

Please just one, thought Cindy.

"WMML, local news has learned exclusively that one of the election officers here at the Chesterbrook precinct has been dismissed for inappropriate activities. Would you care to comment on that?"

Cindy was stunned. How had they heard about that? One of the voters who had been in the gym at the time of Millicent's dismissal must have gone to the news. Just for a moment Cindy's smile was replaced by a countenance of confusion and panic.

"Well—uh—no—what I mean is—each of our officers maintain the highest standards—"

"But clearly this one did not."

"Tracy, you really need to direct any personnel issues to the Office of Elections. I will say emphatically that all of our voters have been treated with the upmost respect and according to law."

"Very nice. Well that's the way it is here at the Chesterbrook precinct. This is Tracy Miller."

The bright light went out. "That was lovely," said Tracy. "Thank you so much. Now I see that the candidate has voted and has left by the side door so I must go as well. Hope to see you again, real soon."

Cindy tried to smile but it was more of a grimace.

Hope to see you again, never, she thought as Tracy and her cameraman headed for the exit.

28

TUESDAY, 7:45 A.M.

THE MINUTES PASSED and the rhythm of the precinct that had begun at 6:00 a.m. continued. The voters remained, for the most part, men and woman who were obviously on their way to work. There were no "exception" situations; no handicapped people who needed special attention; no one who had moved five years prior and forgot to change their registration; no one who seemed uncertain how the voting process worked or uncertain over who would receive their vote. They came; they voted; they left. Carl and Pam checked them in with a minimum of fuss and Jerry provided them with their ballots. Theodore was ready to instruct them on using the scanner but no one seemed to need any help.

And once again Cindy was left to sit and reflect on her performance so far as chief election officer.

"We are on our second pack of one hundred," Jerry had announced at 7:30 as he started to use the ballots that Cindy had counted some forty minutes prior.

Now as the clock approached 8:00 a.m., sounds of life were beginning to be heard from other parts of the school. Teachers could be heard conversing in the hallway and one of the Phys Ed teachers entered the gym and crossed over to his office. Mrs. Martin, the assistant principal, came in, looked around, saw Carl and called out,

"Carl, do you need anything?"

Carl looked over to Cindy. She immediately stared down at some forms on the chief's table.

"No thank you, Mrs. Martin. We're fine."

Cindy was beginning to contemplate rotating the officer assignments on the top of the hour. It was a long day and any election officer, even the best, could get punchy if left in the same assignment for too long. This meant taking Carl and Pam off the EPBs at least for an hour or so which couldn't help but degrade things a bit. Hopefully the 8-to-10 crowd would not be quite as numerous as the early birds.

With only five officers on hand there was a limit to the team's flexibility. Normally the chief did not take a full assignment but rather left herself free for special exception situations and to fill in temporarily when someone needed a break. But with so few officers this was not feasible. She would have to put herself along with Jerry on the EPBs. Pam could take over the ballot table and Carl would work the scanner. Theodore would get a break. She had meant to give him one earlier but never got around to it.

Suddenly a commotion could be heard coming from the hallway just outside the gym.

"You have no standing here. You are not allowed here!" boomed a deep throated male voice.

"I am simply presenting this to the chief. I have a right—," also a male voice but this one was softer, much more conversational.

"Not in here you don't!" came the load rejoinder.

The two men came into view. Cindy immediately recognized the larger of the two as Democratic Party County Chairman Brian "Biff" Logan, whom she had seen a number of times on TV. The other was a slightly built man with graying hair and moustache. The two men approached the EPB check-in table.

"My name is Walter Harrington. I would like to speak to the chief, please," the smaller man said. His tone was polite, almost deferential.

"Make him show you his authorization," said Biff Logan. "He has not been authorized as a poll watcher. He is just a volunteer working outside and has no standing."

Both Carl and Pam looked over toward Cindy who had already heard enough and was heading over to the two men.

"If you two gentlemen would join me at the chief's table, I'm sure we can resolve this situation," said Cindy with an air of calm, businesslike, politeness. They followed her over to the chief's table and each took a seat.

"You have no right to listen to him. He is not authorized. Carl Marsden would have never even let him in the door," proclaimed Biff Logan.

You just said the wrong thing buster, thought Cindy even as she calmly replied, "I will decide who I may listen to." She then turned to Walter.

"What is on your mind sir?"

"This," he declared giving her a flier on letter sized paper. On it was printed a facsimile of the official ballot with the words "Sample Ballot" printed on top and a big checkmark by the name of the Democratic candidate, Emily Weston. Sample ballots were a standard form of party propaganda in elections. Party volunteers would hand them out to voters on their way to the polls in an attempt to show them the "correct" way to vote. They were perfectly legal so long as such activity was done outside the forty foot line. The voter could then take the sample ballot inside the polling place to refer to while voting, so long as it was not shown to other voters.

"It's printed on yellow paper," the man continued. "By law, sample ballots may not be printed on paper that is either white or yellow. It's so they won't be confused with official county documents. These sample ballots are illegal. The Democrats are distributing this ballot right outside the school by the tree. They need to be ordered to halt distribution immediately."

"It's not yellow. It's goldenrod," said Biff. "See right here," he added shoving a paint store catalog in Cindy's face.

"It's yellow," countered Walter.

"It's goldenrod. You have no right to interfere," shouted Biff at Walter. "You try that and we'll sue you into the dark ages."

"And you too Missy," he added, directing his venom at Cindy.

Cindy looked at the paper. She knew about the rule prohibiting white and yellow sample ballots. The paper she held was yellow, sort of. But it did have a hint of orange as well.

Rising to her feet, she said, "If you gentlemen will excuse me for a moment." She then retreated into a corner for a bit of privacy and quickly dialed the Command Center.

"Roger, we have a situation. The Democrats are handing out sample ballots that the Republicans claim are illegal because they are printed on yellow paper."

"Are they?"

"Are they what?"

"Are they printed on yellow paper?"

"I don't know. It's sort of yellow with a bit of orange. But it's not what I think that matters. You guys need to make the call."

"But we don't have the paper. You do."

"But don't we need a countywide decision? I'm sure they are handing them out at the other precincts as well."

"I agree. There needs to be a county wide decision. But we don't have the paper and you do."

"We can take a picture and transmit it."

"Not the same thing."

"So does this mean that you'll poll each of the other precincts to form some sort of consensus."

"That would take up too much time. None of the other precincts have reported it. You're the chief. You have to make the call."

"For the whole county?"

"Yes."

"No Roger, there has to be some other way to resolve this. Shades of color; that's not my thing. I never even took Art 101."

"But you're the chief. It's your call."

A pause and a sigh.

"So let me get this straight. I need to decide whether this thing is yellow or not, using the vast expertise that I acquired playing with coloring books as a kid, and then whatever I decide becomes the official position of the entire county for this election."

"That pretty much says it."

Dear Lord in heaven, thought Cindy. *Send me to the looney bin. No, wait, I'm already there.*

"What if I say I'm color blind?"

"Are you?"

"No, but—"

"Then you're still good to go. Look Cindy, there is one way out if you don't want to personally bear the entire burden. You can take a vote among the election officers at your precinct. Then however the vote comes out, that will decide it."

"Vox Populi"

"Something like that. But we do need a decision pretty quick so take your poll and get back to us."

They said their goodbyes and hung up. Cindy went back to the chief's table.

"Still working on it," she snapped at Walter and Biff even as she grabbed a clipboard from the table. She then attached the sample ballot to the clipboard so that the back side of the paper faced out. A person looking at it would not realize that it was a sample ballot.

She walked over to the ballot table where Jerry had just handed a ballot to a voter.

"Jerry," she said, showing him the paper. "In your opinion is this yellow or is it something else?"

Jerry stared at the paper with interest. "That's a strange question," he declared. "Who wants to know?"

"The entire county."

Jerry considered. "The basic hue is yellow but that orange tint makes it interesting. Most interesting."

Oh no, thought Cindy. *Jerry must be an artist.*

Jerry continued to ponder. "It reminds me a bit of butterfield. Or possibly goldenrod. Maybe even sunflower."

"Jerry, yellow or no?"

Jerry stared at it for a moment more. "It's not yellow," he said slowly. "I'm not sure what it is but it's not yellow."

"Thank you, Jerry," said Cindy, taking back the clipboard. She walked over to Theodore who was seated by the scanner.

"Theodore, is this yellow or is it something else?"

Unlike Jerry, Theodore gave the paper only the briefest of glances.

"I'm a simple man, Cindy. I grew up with the basic Crayola 8-crayon box. It's yellow."

She thanked Theodore and proceeded over to the EPB table. She showed it to Pam first.

Pam smiled. "I bet Jerry had fun with this. He likes to dabble with painting, you know."

She considered the paper for a few moments and then declared, "It's a variation of yellow but it's still yellow."

Cindy then walked around the table to Carl, assuming a demeanor of rigid formality. This would be the first time she would be speaking directly to him since the incident with Millicent over an hour ago.

"Carl," she said crisply. "I need your opinion. Is this yellow or is it something else?"

Carl looked at the paper. "So the Democrats are at it again," he said. "They do this every few years. But whenever it's happened in the past, I would always kick it up to the Command Center for a decision."

"Well, they've kicked it back to us," replied Cindy.

"Actually, that makes sense," he said reflecting on the situation. "The only precincts voting today are at least twenty miles from the Government Center. In the past this always came up during a November election when all the precincts are open. So they could have easily got hold of one of the papers from a nearby—"

"Carl, dispense with the backstory. Is it yellow or not?"

Carl stared intently at the paper. "It really is a borderline call," he said more to himself than to Cindy. "Generally if something is a borderline call, I prefer to err on the side of permissiveness."

He looked up at Cindy. "Not yellow."

Cindy took back the clipboard, gave him a curt nod, and walked away. Once she was safely by herself, she reflected on her situation. The vote was 2 to 2. Her attempt to avoid being the decision maker had failed. She had to admit that there was a certain amount of grim humor in that. She also had to admit that she tended to agree with Carl's logic. Except when personal safety was involved, she leaned toward permissiveness in borderline situations. She quickly dialed the Government Center.

"Roger, by the overwhelming vote of 3 to 2, the Chesterbrook precinct has ruled that the sample ballot is not yellow so pending any alternative direction from you, we will not interfere with it being used."

"Thank you, Cindy. That wasn't too painful, was it?"

"Good bye, Roger."

Cindy then returned to the ballot table.

"Gentlemen, I apologize for keeping you so long. A decision has been made that the sample ballot is not yellow and may be use—"

"I knew it!" cried Biff, pumping his first into the air. "You just saved yourself a lawsuit Missy."

With that, Biff marched out of the room.

"Walter, I'm sorry—" Cindy began.

"Don't be," said Walter. "You gave us a fair hearing."

"Walter, excuse me but I have to ask. Don't you guys have more substantial things to argue about than the color of fliers? You know, like national security or something?"

Walter chuckled. "Oh we argue about that, too. Anyway I've got to get outside and hand out our sample ballots. Which are blue by the way."

Walter got up to leave. As he exited, static started coming from the radio.

"Attention all chiefs; Attention all chief's. One of the political parties is handing out a sample ballot which has been challenged because it is allegedly printed on yellow paper. After careful analysis the Office of Elections has determined that the paper is not yellow and may be used. Repeat, it may be used."

29

TUESDAY 8:15 A.M.

"PAM, WHAT'S THE pollbook count right now?" asked Cindy. "It is exactly 138," said Pam looking at the screen.

"Which matches what I want it to be. Thanks a bunch. I know I need to rotate you guys. That 'Is it yellow?' conundrum set me back. I'll record this in the log and get back to you."

Cindy hurried off to the chief's table to make her entries in the log.

"She really is trying, you know," said Pam to Carl.

Before he could respond, a gray haired lady who had just entered the gym came up to the EPB table. She presented herself before Carl.

"Eleanor Phyllis Mclemore." Her voice seemed to quiver with anticipation.

"Very good Ms. Mclemore. May I see your ID?"

"Let's see, I have it here somewhere," she said. "I'm really excited about this election. We are going to decide which party controls the Senate. And we all know what party that will be." She gave Carl a sly wink.

"Yes ma'am. Your ID, please."

"Here it is. I found it. Would you like to see my driver's license or my concealed gun permit?" She patted her handbag and gave a knowing smile. Carl didn't dare ask.

"Your driver's license would be fine."

"I can show you both."

"Just the driver's license if you please."

Ms. Mclemore handed the license to Carl. He confirmed that the photo on the license appeared to be that of the lady in front of him.

Carl then entered the name into the EPB. It was not found.

"Ma'am, how do you spell your name?"

"M-c-l-e-m-o-r-e"

He entered it again. Nothing. He tried it with a blank after the c. He tried it with an apostrophe instead of the c. He was unable to find any Eleanor Mclemore in the pollbook.

"I'm sorry ma'am but I'm not finding you. What is your address?"

"4880 Ridge Road."

Carl considered. After five years of being chief, he knew most of the streets in the Chesterbrook precinct but Ridge Road did not ring a bell.

"Let me try something else," he said. He used the mouse to slide an on-screen bubble from "precinct" to "all."

"Now I can search the entire county and there it is. Why Ms. Mclemore, you are in the Gunderson precinct. They are not voting today."

"I know; that's why I'm here. This is where the action is. The sign outside says 'Vote Here' and I'm here to vote."

"But I'm afraid you're not registered here. You are already represented in the State Senate."

"Yes, I know. He's that nice little man who always runs unopposed. But he's not running today. In fact there's nothing going on over at Gunderson. That's why I figured I'd come over here."

"I'm afraid ma'am it doesn't work that way. We all get to vote only in the precinct where we live. Otherwise everyone would be crisscrossing the state looking for the most interesting races. And there would be no one left in Gunderson to vote for that nice little man. Surely you see that ma'am?"

Ms. Mclemore gave a sigh reflecting her disappointment. "Well if you put it this way, I suppose so. I do think it's a shame though. Well, have a good day." She turned and walked out of the gym.

While this exchange had been going on, Cindy had come up behind the table. With Ms. Mclemore's exit, it was time to rotate the officers.

"Pam, do you need a break?" she asked.

"Not right now, thanks," replied Pam.

"OK, then why don't you go back and work the ballot table. Tell Jerry that he can take a quick break and then join me with the EPBs. Carl, you take the scanner and tell Theodore to take a break. I think he needs it."

Pam went back to the ballot table. She exchanged a quick word with Jerry who then got up and left the gym for the restroom. Cindy sat down at the table and signaled for the next voter in line. Out of the corner of her eye she noticed that Carl had not left his seat.

"May I make a suggestion?" he asked rather stiffly.

Cindy gave the slightest of nods.

"Let me stay here until Jerry gets back. We've got a line and it will only get longer if we have only one person checking in the voters. When Jerry gets back, I'll go to the scanner and relieve Theodore. I think he can last a few more minutes."

There was silence for a few seconds. Finally Cindy said "OK," barely above a whisper and without looking in Carl's direction.

For the next several minutes they worked side-by-side checking in voters. Although Carl was primarily focused on processing the voters in front of him, he could tell that Cindy seemed well versed in the check-in process. She processed the voters with a business-like cordiality that was most efficient and the line actually began to shrink a little. Whatever her deficiencies as overall chief might be, she had obviously absorbed the mechanics of the check-in process. Eventually Jerry came back from his break and Carl went back to relieve Theodore.

"Theodore, Cindy wants you to take a break," he said to an appreciative Theodore who left the gym in search of the restroom.

Theodore is delicate, thought Carl. *I hope Cindy realizes that.*

Working the scanner was one of the easier Election Day duties. The slot where the ballot was inserted was fairly obvious and most of the time the officer was left with little to do besides point at the slot and hand out "I Voted" stickers. This left Carl with time to look over the whole operation and reflect on how the morning had been going.

As he gazed over the gym, he had to admit that the precinct seemed to be in pretty good shape in spite of the various incidents that had occurred that morning. At the EPB table, Jerry wasn't as efficient as Pam but Cindy was processing them like a pro and between the two of them the line seemed to be leveling out. Pam had the ballot table well in hand; Theodore had done a good job with the signs; yes, things seemed to be going well.

On the other hand, the fact that the chief and assistant chief were barely speaking to each other was not good. Carl wished he could say something to at least thaw things out a little but for now Cindy seemed determined to keep her distance. That episode with Millicent was apparently for her, the last straw. The truth was that he had also found it painful that Millicent had to be sent home. He wished he could find some way to make Cindy understand that he appreciated the pain of the situation.

Carl suddenly became aware of a decided chill in the room. Looking over at the side exit door he realized why. The last voter had opened the door to its full extent when leaving and it had remained open. He quickly went over to close the door. Besides letting in the cold air, an open door could suggest to people coming up the walkway that this was an entrance.

Carl reached the door and stepped outside to look around. Dawn had arrived and the sun was trying to shine through. He looked at the sky where cirrus clouds, "mares' tails," seemed to be everywhere, suggesting that a weather event was not too far away. The temperature was definitely above freezing, perhaps the mid-40s, but Carl had heard that it would be dropping later in the day.

He then looked down the side walkway that led to the parking lot where individual voters were coming from. The Democrats had set up a table with campaign literature while the Republicans had contented themselves with having their literature on a folding chair. Party operatives were handing out their sample ballots; some blue, others "goldenrod." Carl smiled at that. Cindy had actually handled the controversy of the yellow sample ballots rather well.

To the left he saw the main walkway coming from the front sidewalk. By the tree, marking the forty foot boundary, both parties had set up tables with campaign literature. Behind that was a driveway where the first school buses of the day were arriving.

Suddenly Carl realized that something was wrong. The tables by the tree were fine, forty feet from the front door, no problem. But what about all that campaigning on the side walkway? They were well over forty feet from the front entrance where people entered but what about this side exit door? In the past this door had not been used on Election Day at all so it was not a factor; they had not even counted it as an entrance but now that it was in use, even as just an exit, the situation had changed.

Carl realized that it wasn't his place to direct those people to evacuate their positions. But it was the chief's; it was Cindy's. He went back inside and closed the door to keep out the cold. Sitting off to one side was Theodore, enjoying his break.

"Theodore, could you take the scanner for a couple of minutes?" he asked. "I need to talk to our chief."

"I've got it. Take all the time you need."

Carl walked quickly over to the EPB table to where Cindy was processing a voter.

"Phillip Voorhees Washington, 51 Tyler Drive. Here is your ballot card. If you take it to the ballot table over there you will receive your ballot—what is it Carl?"

"We need to talk."

Cindy gave him a long, hard stare. Carl stared right back.

"Very well. Jerry, you're on your own for a couple of minutes."

Carl thought that it would probably take more than a couple of minutes but decided that it was best not to articulate that.

"OK Carl, you have my attention. What is it?" said Cindy. Her brusque tone suggested that "this better be important."

"Both parties are outside campaigning within the forty foot line."

She frowned. "I thought you said that everyone knew about the tree."

"The tree is not the problem. It's that door," said Carl, pointing to the exit door.

"I don't understand."

"It goes like this," he began. "Prior to this election we never used that door. It was always shut so the Command Center allowed us to consider that door as not being an entrance. So we did not worry about folks campaigning within forty feet of it. We only worried about the front door. Now however, the door is being used. So the forty foot limit applies and poll workers are doing their thing within that limit. They need to be removed."

"No, they don't," Cindy retorted. "That door is an exit, not an entrance. The only people walking through that door have already voted."

"It doesn't matter whether people are entering or exiting. The door is still functioning as an entrance to the polling place. Let me get the manual and I'll show you."

Carl retrieved the manual from the chief's table and quickly found the relevant section. It stated, "Campaigners must remain at least forty feet away from any entrance to the building in which the polling place is located."

Cindy studied the page.

"See, I'm not making it up. Call the Command Center if you want to," said Carl.

"No. That's not necessary," said Cindy. "The language is plain enough."

"So you will have them move?"

"No, Carl. You will."

"But you're the chief."

"Yes, I am the chief," said Cindy, who suddenly took on a rather formal bearing. "And as chief of this precinct I am giving you an assignment. I am directing you, the assistant chief, to go outside and round up those heinous lawbreakers and herd them along with their supplies back across the forty foot line and please do it as quickly as possible before the republic crumbles. Now if you will excuse me, I have voters to check in." And with that she turned back to face the line which had grown a bit since she had gone offline to talk with Carl.

Armed with this, somewhat sarcastically given, directive from his chief Carl headed for the exit door. Opening the door, he decided that rather than approach the poll workers individually, he would issue a global directive and get it done all at once.

"Party poll workers, I need your attention please," he called out. "I'm afraid you have to conduct your activities at least forty feet away from this door. It's an entrance to the building and the law applies."

"But you've always allowed us to campaign here before," said a Republican who was handing out his blue sample ballots. Carl recognized him by face, as one of the regular poll workers at the precinct.

"I realize that," said Carl. "But this door had always remained shut in prior elections so it wasn't regarded as an entrance. For this election it is being used so you will have to move."

"What's going on here?" It was Biff Logan who had come over from the tree where he had been campaigning.

"We have to relocate to forty feet away from the door," said one of the Democrats who had been handing out their goldenrod fliers.

"Nothing doing," stormed Biff. "We have a right to be here. That door is an exit, not an entrance. This is overreach. Try to move us and we'll sue."

"It doesn't matter that it's an exit," replied Carl firmly. "The rule applies to any entrance to the building, no matter what its use."

The Republican campaigners began to gather up their things and move back toward the tree. The Democrats stood still, waiting for direction from Biff.

"We're not budging," sneered Biff. "Even if what you're saying is true, you don't have the authority to move us. You're not the chief. If Little Miss Coed wants us out of here, she will have to come out herself."

"Little Miss Coed has a name," said a voice from behind Carl. "It's Cynthia Phelps, chief election officer for the Chesterbrook precinct. For now you may call me Ms. Phelps."

Cindy then proceeded to walk past Carl and went up directly to Biff.

"Mr. Logan, you and your people are in violation of sections 24.2-604 and 24.2-310 of the Virginia Election code. I am directing you to cease these illegal activities and remove yourselves to at least forty feet from this door. I am further directing the assistant chief, Mr. Carl Marsden, to remain here until you have complied with the law. Anything he says now or at any other time today should be considered to have come from me. Is that understood?"

Biff glared at Cindy for a few seconds. Then with a shrug he turned to his poll workers. "Come on. Let's move."

Cindy walked back to where Carl was standing. She reached into her jacket pocket and handed Carl her tape measure.

"Mr. Marsden," she said, loudly enough to be heard by the poll workers. "Once they have moved, you will use this tape measure to satisfy yourself that they are in full compliance with the law. Is that understood?"

"Completely, Ms. Phelps," said Carl who then whispered, "and thank you."

"Are you happy now?" she whispered back.

"It's not about me being happy. It's about the rules and procedures that need to be—"

"Oh, bite me," snapped Cindy, no longer in a whisper, as she spun around and went back into the gym.

30

Tuesday, 8:50 a.m.

It took a while for the party poll workers to comply with Cindy's directive. Using her tape measure and some hastily gathered sticks, Carl was able to delineate a forty foot arc that the campaigners relocated to, some with good humor, others less so. When he was at last satisfied, Carl returned to the gym.

It was pretty much as he had left it. Theodore was at the scanner, Pam at the ballot table, and Jerry doing the EPB check-ins. The one exception was Cindy who was now seated at the table on which the "Create Ballot" marking machine was placed. Beside her, seated as well, was an elderly gentleman. His walker was over by the side of the table.

Carl recognized the man, although not by name. For the past few years he had helped him cast his ballot. There was a tremor in his hands that made it very difficult for him to fill in the ovals on the preprinted ballot. Carl would always have the man fill out the *Request for Assistance* form which would then allow him to actually mark the man's ballot, following his instructions of course. From the look of things, Cindy was trying to get him to use the "Create

Ballot" machine to create his ballot, thereby preserving some of his sense of independence.

"Carl," called Pam. "I've only got about ten ballots left. Can you get me the next stack of one hundred?"

Carl nodded and went over to Cindy. The man she was talking to seemed a bit agitated.

"So you must explain again. How does this machine work?" he was asking.

"Excuse me Cindy. Pam needs the next pack of one hundred."

"Here's the key to the cart. Could you get the next pack and help Pam with the counting?" she responded.

"Hello Carl," said the man. "You helped me vote last year. This girl wants me to use this machine but I don't know."

"Well you're in good hands, sir," replied Carl. "She will guide you well."

Cindy gave Carl a quizzical expression as if she wasn't sure whether he was being sarcastic or sincere.

Carl hurried over to the cart. He could hear Cindy explaining how the machine worked, apparently for the second time.

Using the key he unlocked the cart, extracted the next pack of ballots, and spent the following ten minutes verifying the count. As he was doing this, he noticed that the line at the check-in table was growing longer. This was unusual. Most of the time by 9:00 a.m. the early birds, on their way to work, would have come and gone. There would be fewer voters and hence fewer lines. The problem here was that Jerry was by himself at the check-in table. Cindy was still over at the "Create Ballot" table with the man who seemed to be getting more and more frustrated.

Carl had just made up his mind to go to the check-in table to help Jerry when Cindy came over to him. She looked concerned, even a bit harried.

"Carl, I can't get the 'Create Ballot' to work. The correct screen comes up and the gentleman can enter his selection but at the end of the process, it just returns the blank card without anything on it."

"Let's take a look."

"So much trouble. This machine is so much trouble," the man was saying as they approached.

Cindy inserted the blank card. From Carl's vantage point she was doing it correctly. Once the machine accepted the blank card, the voter would see a touch screen display of the ballot. He would push his selections on the screen and the machine would print the marked ballot which would then be fed into the scanner.

"Now Mr. Samuels, could you try entering your selections again," said Cindy, retreating so as to give him some privacy.

"I did this already," said the obviously frustrated Mr. Samuels who nonetheless began to make his selection on the machine.

"Let us know when you are finished," said Cindy.

After a minute Mr. Samuels asserted. "I see my selection on the screen. It shows my selection, Jennifer Haley. There is a square that says 'Print Ballot.' This is where I was before."

"OK, press the square."

Mr. Samuels complied. The machine then emitted the card, just as blank as when it had been entered.

"Two things," said Carl, pulling Cindy aside so they could converse in relative privacy. "First, this machine is malfunctioning. I'd put it away and set up the other machine you have in the cart. Then call Milton to see if he has a replacement. Secondly, I really don't think this man wants to use the machine. I would recommended you offering to assist him instead."

"The other machine is also defective. It failed to boot up this morning."

"Did you tell Milton?"

A pause.

"No I did not. In our panic over the EPBs, it slipped my mind."

"Then I would call him as soon as you can. But first get this man squared away." Carl tried to make his tone conversational, rather than as an accusation. Cindy glared at Carl for a brief moment. Apparently his conciliatory tone hadn't registered.

Turning back to the man, Cindy said, "Mr. Samuels, we're having a bit of a problem with the machine so why don't we fill out a *Request for Assistance* form and then I can help you mark the ballot exactly as you would like it."

Mr. Samuels thought for a moment and then lifted his hand and pointed at Carl. "I want him. He's helped me before. I want him to help me now."

Cindy and Carl exchanged glances. For the briefest instant Carl thought he saw a reaction from Cindy over her obvious rejection. But she recovered so quickly that he decided that he must have imagined it.

"Of course. Carl why don't you get one of the *Request for Assistance* forms from the chief's table and help Mr. Samuels get squared away? It was a pleasure meeting you Mr. Samuels."

31

TUESDAY, 9:10 A.M.

"**M**ILTON, THIS IS Cindy over at Chesterbrook. I have to re-port that both our 'Create Ballot' machines have mal-functioned. The first one failed to boot up this morning. Some sort of 'test error.' The other one accepts the card and allows the voter to make his selection but then returns a blank card at the end of the process."

"It sounds like neither machine is going to do you any good. They will be sent back to the manufacturer. Fortunately they are still under warranty."

"Where does that leave us today?"

"Without a 'Create Ballot' machine, I'm afraid. They did not issue me any backups. You'll just have to process all the handi-capped voters with the *Request for Assistance* form."

"That's what I sort of expected."

"Sorry. But now that I have you on the line, I have a question for you. I need some advice and I've been told that you're the one person in the county with the expertise I need."

"Ask away," said Cindy, rather perplexed that Milton would be asking her for advice about anything.

"You see my wife wants me to repaint the kitchen so I'd like your opinion. Should I go with yellow or would goldenrod be a better choice? Or maybe sunflower?"

Cindy was not amused.

"Ha. Ha. Very funny. I hope they're not paying you for your wit."

"Perhaps butterfield?"

"Milton, stuff it. Are we going to see you again soon?"

"Not for a while, I'm afraid. I'm still on the first go round. Hagerman has called me back twice for various issues. How are you all doing?"

"Understaffed and taking our lumps but we're still standing."

"Way to be. See you soon."

Upon hanging up, Cindy looked over at the EPB table which brought her back to reality in a flash. Jerry had been doing the check-ins by himself and he was overwhelmed. The line stretched out across the gym to the door. Cindy hurried over to the EPB table, sat next to Jerry, and started to work, processing voters. She realized that she was missing her 9:00 a.m. voter count log entry but it could not be helped. They were really understaffed.

Carl came over. "Mr. Samuels has voted. Where do you want me?"

"Right here," said Cindy, pointing to Jerry's chair. "Jerry you go back to the ballot table and relieve Pam. Order her to take a break. She hasn't had a rest yet."

For the next twenty minutes they worked side by side checking in voters in an attempt to get the line down to a manageable level. These voters were a slightly different breed from the "early bird to work" lot that had voted the first couple of hours. Mothers with their small children in tow were now more prevalent.

In the meantime the rhythm of the school began to be felt. Announcements came over the loudspeaker. *"Due to our standardized testing there will be no Art, Music, or PE classes."; "We will now say the Pledge of Allegiance."; "There is a car blocking the main driveway."*

Occasionally a student would stick his head through the gym door and look around in wonder. What are all these strange old people doing in our school?

"Yes, I know but the board doesn't meet until Thursday so we still have time."

The man standing before Cindy, wearing a business suit, appeared to be in his forties. He was turned to one side and was speaking rather loudly into his cell phone.

"Well that's what I mean. Get the ball rolling now."

"Excuse me, sir," interjected Cindy. "I need you to state your full legal name. And you really shouldn't be talking on your cell phone. It is a distraction."

"What?" said the man. It wasn't clear if he was responding to Cindy or the person he was talking to on his cell.

"I need your full legal name," said Cindy. "And I need you to complete your phone call now."

"What? No, that was just some clerk. I'm on line to vote. OK, we'll talk later. Bye." The man put away to his cell phone and turned to face Cindy, a look of mild annoyance on his face.

"I need to have your full legal name," she repeated, flashing what she hoped was her best smile.

"Carson. Tom Carson."

Cindy doubted if that was his full name but decided not to press it.

"May I see your ID please?"

Mr. Carson produced his driver's license. The photo on it checked out.

She entered the name "Carson" into the EPB.

A number of Carsons appeared on the screen but there was no Thomas or Tom.

"Sir, I'm having trouble finding you in the system. Could you tell me your full legal name?"

The man took an exaggerated deep breath and rolled his eyes.

"Thomas Stuart Carson. Can you speed this up a bit miss? I really have important things to take care of."

"And your address sir."

"It's right there on my ID. 32 Baker Court."

Once again Cindy stared at the screen.

"I do see a Helen Carson at 32 Baker Court. She appears to have already voted today."

"Yeah, that's my wife. What is the problem? Do you need me to help you with your laptop?" Cindy could tell that Mr. Carson was getting agitated.

"Sir, may I ask, when was the last time you voted?"

"Oh I don't know. The last presidential, I think."

"Did you vote here?"

"Of course not. We were living in Newport News at the time. We moved here this past summer. We did our address change at the DMV. So now we live here. End of Story."

"It would appear," said Cindy, trying to choose her words carefully, "that your wife's address change made it into the system but yours did not. Now I am going to call—"

"What! That is not acceptable. We filled out our paperwork at the DMV at exactly the same time. I have a constitutional right to vote and no little functionary like you is going to stop me."

Cindy was desperately trying to stay calm. She was perfectly comfortable battling the Biff Logans of the world but this was different. However annoying Mr. Carson might be, he was still part of the public that she had sworn to serve and it was beginning to appear that he might have been the victim of some bureaucratic mix-up.

"Mr. Carson," she said. "I will do everything I can to help you. If you come back with me, I will call the Office of Elections and we can get this thing straightened out."

With that Cindy rose and gestured for him to follow her back to the chief's table. She also motioned to Pam who had just returned from her break. Pam immediately understood and went to take her vacated place at the check-in table.

"Have a seat Mr. Carson," said Cindy, taking a seat herself at the chief's table. Taking out a Voter Referral worksheet, she wrote down his name and address.

"I do need the last four digits of your social security number."

"And why should I give personal information like that to a complete stranger?"

"I need to provide that information to the Government Center so they can track down your registration," replied Cindy. A note of pleading had crept into her voice, Mr. Carson was beginning to wear her down.

"I'm going to lodge a complaint when this is over. What is your name?"

"My name is Cynthia Phelps. I am the chief election officer for the—"

"Well Miss Phelps. We'll see how long that lasts."

Cindy picked up her phone and dialed the Government Center registration phone number.

"Voter registration. Naomi speaking."

"Hi. This is Cindy Phelps over at Chesterbrook. I have a voter who is not on our roles. He swears he registered his address change with the DMV. His wife registered the same day and she is in the system."

"What's the Social?"

"He's reluctant to give it to me."

"It really helps if we have at least the last four digits."

Looking up at Mr. Carson, Cindy said, "They really need the last four digits Mr. Carson. If you want this to go any further, we need to have them."

With his face expressing extreme displeasure, Mr. Carson provided the number which Cindy passed along to Naomi along with his name.

"Let's see. I am finding a Thomas Stuart Carson with those last four digits. He is registered to vote in Newport News."

"He says he did an address change with the DMV."

"Could be. He may have failed to initial the box on the DMV form that says change my voter address as well. Or the DMV may have screwed up. Anyway have him do a provisional ballot. If we can track down that DMV form in the next couple of days, his vote might count. And have him fill out a new voter registration form as well to protect him for future elections even if this one doesn't pan out."

Cindy thanked Naomi and they completed the call. She then took a moment to steel herself for the conversation ahead. This was not going to be pleasant.

"Mr. Carson," she said, trying to sound calm, businesslike, and sympathetic all at the same time. "You are listed on the database at your old Newport News address."

"What! I don't believe this! I do not believe this!"

For the next few minutes Mr. Carson railed on against the incompetent Office of Elections and especially Cindy who were trampling on his constitutional rights. This was also beginning to attract the attention of others in the gym and especially the party poll watchers who seemed to be most interested in what was happening.

Once he appeared to have said his mind, Cindy continued. "There are two things I can do for you. First you can fill out a provisional ballot. In three days the Office of Elections examines the provisional ballots and determines whether they will be counted. During that time they will make an attempt to locate your DMV form. If they can determine that you initialed the elections box they will count your vote. Secondly we will have you fill out a new registration form. Then regardless of how today's events play out, you will be registered for future elections."

It was obvious that Mr. Carson did not think much of the plan but he also realized that he had no choice.

"This is totally unacceptable," he proclaimed. "And I will be filing a complaint."

"Yes sir," said Cindy. "Now if you just bear with me."

Cindy opened her manual to the section on provisional ballots.

"I have not done one of these before and I want to be sure that I—"

Even as she was saying those words, Cindy realized that she was making a mistake.

"You haven't done this before," interrupted Mr. Carson, amazement on his face. "So now I have to sit here and wait until you figure this all out. Is this how the county conducts its elections? It's a nightmare. A complete nightmare!"

"Excuse me." It was Carl.

"Cindy," he said, "I've done lots of provisionals. If you'd like, I can take over from here."

Cindy looked up at Carl, trying hard not to look as helpless and vulnerable as she felt. She nodded and got up.

"I'm taking a break," she said quietly to Carl. "You're in charge until I get back."

Then, as quickly as possible, she walked out of the gym, hoping that no one would notice the tears in her eyes.

32

TUESDAY, 9:45 A.M.

CINDY NEEDED TO be alone if only for a few minutes. Finding such a place in an elementary school that's in session was not that easy but eventually she found a small nook in back of the school next to the dumpster. There in relative privacy she allowed herself to break down. She could not recall ever having felt so inadequate and the sensation overwhelmed her. For a few minutes she just stood there, trembling slightly, her arms wrapped tightly together, as tears ran down her face.

As she slowly regained her composure she reached into her handbag. She fished around for a few seconds, finally getting her fingers around the pack of cigarettes that she had buried near the bottom. She had given up smoking after leaving college but still kept a pack for "special situations."

And this is about as special as it gets, she thought, lighting up. Hoping that it would help settle her down, she took a deep drag.

"Yuck. I can't believe I did this all through college."

Cindy then pondered her situation. She had become used to her life being one success after another. She actually enjoyed having to prove herself. Her looks, personality, and quick wit made her a winner in just about everything she attempted.

That's what made what she was experiencing all the more unsettling. What she originally had expected would be a mild diversion had turned into something that threatened to overwhelm her.

I need to turn this around, she thought. *But how?*

She had already acknowledged that her preparation had begun late and had not been as thorough as it should have been. In addition her inexperience had hurt in a number of ways from the botched interview with Tracy to the most recent provisional ballot snafu.

And then there was her frayed relationship with the assistant chief.

Carl was clearly the master of all this election "stuff." He obviously resented her taking over as chief. His tendency to talk down to her along with his slavish obsession with the rules had been a source of continual friction between them. But Cindy also realized that she had made it worse, much worse in fact, than it had to be. Carl seemed to have brought out the petty side of her character, a side that she was usually able to keep in check. In her zealousness to assert and maintain her position as chief, she had created a wall between her and the one person who could best help her through this day. She would have to do what she could to establish at least some sort of connection.

But there was more to it than merely trying to get access to Carl's expertise. It was apparent that he had very little respect for Cindy and this genuinely bothered her. She wasn't sure why it was so important that Carl respect her. She wasn't particularly attracted to him (well perhaps just a little). All she knew was that it was. And she knew that the only way she would achieve it would come from applying every bit of her intellect and tenacity into doing the job right. Charm by itself would not get it done.

Neither will I get it done standing out here by the dumpster, she reflected. *Time to get back in the game.* Crushing out her cigarette, she went back into the school.

33

TUESDAY, 10:00 A.M.

"*B*ASE, EASTHAMPTON IS *checking in with 232 votes cast*"
"*Copy that, Easthampton. You are the first to report.*"

"Cindy, where have you been?" called Carl, rather annoyed. "They've started the ten o'clock call in with vote totals."

"OK, I'm on it," she said, hurrying back to the chief's table. She needed to get the 10:00 a.m. numbers in her log first, having missed recording the numbers at 9:00 a.m.

"*Base, this is Danby checking in at 204.*"

"*Copy that, Danby. Thanks.*"

With the log in hand Cindy hurried over to the scanner where Pam was.

"Pam, what's our count on the scanner?"

"Let's see. We are at 267. So we are in first place so far."

"I didn't know it was a competition."

"It's not of course. Still we do take a bit of pride in our precinct and getting a good turnout."

"*Base, this is Manchester. The biggest and the best checking in with 384 voters.*"

"*Copy that, Manchester. Great job.*"

Cindy and Pam exchanged glances. "Well they're bigger than we are," said Pam weakly.

Cindy looked over the gym. There was one voter marking his ballot, two in line at the ballot table and one checking in. *So the EPB count should be 271*, she thought.

"Base, Seneca Grove has 188 voters."

"Copy that, Seneca Grove. Good hearing from you."

Cindy hurried toward the EPB table where Carl and Theodore were seated.

"Base, this is Wallingford. We have 213 voters."

"Copy that, Wallingford. Thanks for the update."

Cindy deliberately went over to Carl's side of the table.

"What's our EPB count, Carl?"

"Let's see; it's 271."

"Which is what it should be. Thanks."

She started back to the chief's table where the radio was.

"We're waiting on Hagerman, Chesterbrook, and Cooper."

"Base this is Hagerman," came the high pitched voice. *"We have 402 voters. No wait…It's 204. We have 204 voters."*

"Copy that, Hagerman. Thank you. Chesterbrook and Cooper we need to hear from you."

Cindy picked up the radio. *"Base, Chesterbrook forges into second place with 271 voters."*

"Copy that, Chesterbrook. I didn't know it was a competition but thanks anyway."

Cindy flashed a look at Pam who smiled and shrugged.

"Cooper, where are you?"

Having discharged her communication responsibility, Cindy sat down and opened her manual to the section on provisional ballots and began reading. She was not going to be blindsided by this again. For the next ten minutes she studied the section, committing significant portions to memory. Every minute or so she would be distracted by a,

"Cooper, we need those vote totals." coming from the radio.

Finally, at just about the time when Cindy could, with confidence say that she knew the provisional ballot procedure, the voice of Julia Hopkins came over the radio. She spoke very slowly.

"Base, this is Cooper. I am sorry that I am late. We have 226 voters at Cooper. Repeat 226 voters at Cooper."

"Copy that, Cooper. Great to hear from you. To all chiefs; to all chiefs. Thank you for your 10:00 a.m. numbers. Your next call in will be at 2:00 p.m."

Focused as she was on her own situation, Cindy still felt empathy for Julia. It sounded like she was struggling. Cindy hoped she had a good team behind her.

Reflecting on her own team, she realized that there was one move she had to make. Once again she walked over to the EPB table.

"Carl, I'm taking your place here at the check-in table. You need to take a break."

He looked up. "I don't need a break. I'm fine."

"Carl, you're the only one on the team that has not had a break. As chief I am ordering you to take one. See me in fifteen minutes and I'll figure out where you go next."

He made a face of displeasure but slowly got to his feet and walked away.

You're not making it easy, thought Cindy, taking her seat next to Theodore.

The activity at the check-in table was not as intense as it had been earlier. The "in a hurry to get to work" crowd had been replaced by what could be best described as the "active retirees." Some wore jogging suits. Others had tennis racquets under their arms. A number were husband-wife duos. A few were acquaintances of Theodore and they would linger and chat for a few minutes.

One of the voters checking in with Cindy had forgotten his ID. The expression that his wife made suggested that this was not a first time occurrence. Cindy explained that the man could either go back to his home and retrieve it or vote a provisional ballot. The man chose to go back and left with his wife. Fifteen minutes later they returned and this time they were checked in.

For the first time since the polls opened, there were actual "breaks" in the line. Periods of a few minutes when there were no voters at all to be processed.

"So how are you enjoying being chief?" asked Theodore during one of these breaks.

"It's a bit overwhelming," said Cindy, truthfully. There was something about Theodore's quiet, unassuming nature that made him easy to talk to. "There's just so much."

"You're doing fine," he said with a smile. "Just remember that you take an oath that says you'll do your best. You don't take an oath that says you'll never make a mistake."

"Tell that to Carl," said Cindy.

"I don't have to," said Theodore. "He's the one who told it to me."

Theodore continued, "Five years ago my wife had just died and for the first time in over fifty years I was alone. I wondered if I would ever be useful again. I volunteered for election duty just for something to pass the time. Carl patiently explained to me each task that he asked me to do. Then when he felt I had mastered it he would move me on to something else. By the end of the day I felt that I had made a real contribution. That helped give me the confidence to volunteer for other causes. Today my schedule is fuller than it was when I was working. I'm not saying that Carl made it all possible but he sure helped get me started."

"He resents me."

"Possibly. No one enjoys being demoted. But mostly he believes deeply in the electoral process. I think we all do."

Cindy said nothing. *"What do I believe in?"* she asked herself, not for the first time. She believed in her own success certainly. And in the importance of doing things well. But beyond that, she wasn't sure. She wished that she could be more idealistic and envied those that were. She had even recently started going back to church, for the first time since middle school. Somehow it was comforting being surrounded by people who apparently knew what they believed in, even if she hadn't a clue herself.

"OK, I'm back." It was Carl.

"Good, you take Theodore's place here. Theodore why don't you take a break?" Theodore thanked her and went off in in pursuit of the restroom.

For the next several minutes Carl and Cindy worked together at the EPB table processing voters and exchanging formalities when required.

"And here we have the actual room where the voting takes place."

Cindy recognized that voice. She looked up just in time to see Biff Logan leading a parade of about twenty individuals. One of Biff's followers was a woman who was rapidly speaking to the group in Spanish.

Carl looked at Cindy. "Are we expecting visitors?"

Her mind raced to recall. "Yes, there is a group from the Brazilian legislature that is supposed to visit the precinct sometime today. It was in the memo that they sent to the chiefs yesterday."

"It would be nice if you let your assistant chief know about such things," said Carl caustically. "This might just fall under the 'absolutely necessary' criteria that you seem to feel is so needed."

"And this is where the poll watchers for the political parties sit. It is their job to ensure that the clerks checking in the voters adhere to all the proper procedures," Biff was continuing. People waiting in line to vote were turning around with interest to see who these newcomers were.

"In the meantime, it would appear that the Democratic Chairman has hijacked the tour," said Carl. "You might want to try establishing your authority."

Cindy was on her feet in a flash. She had already endured two confrontations with Biff and she realized that she needed to assert herself.

"Mr. Logan," Cindy said trying to radiate a confidence she did not feel. "Thank you so much for escorting our guests into the voting area. However before they can observe, I will need to give them a brief introduction to our voting process, outside in the hallway where it won't disturb our voters."

"Oh, that won't be necessity," said Biff. "I've pretty much covered everything with them."

"As chief election officer, it is my responsibility to ensure that our guests have an opportunity to observe our process without upsetting the normal business of our precinct."

"How dare you suggest that our special guests are disrupting the flow of the precinct!" boomed Biff, more for the translator's benefit than for Cindy's.

"They are not disrupting the precinct but you are Mr. Logan and I am ordering you to leave the premises at once." Even as she spoke, Cindy realized that she was taking a big chance. The rules specified that a person could be removed for disrupting a precinct only by a majority of the election officers. Cindy prayed that Biff did not know this as she wasn't positive that Carl would support her. All she knew was that it was not Biff's place to be escorting the Brazilians. If it was anyone's it was hers.

Cindy then turned to the translator. "Please allow me to introduce myself. I am Cynthia Phelps the chief election officer of the Chesterbrook precinct. If you would step outside into the hall I would be happy to provide you all with an overview of what is happening here so you may better appreciate what you see."

The translator hesitated. She realized, as the Brazilians did not, that they were in the midst of a power struggle between Biff Logan, who had guided them thus far, and Cindy.

Biff was about to say something in retaliation, but before he could get the words out, another voice intervened.

"I think you better leave, Mr. Logan," said Carl, with an air of quiet authority.

Biff looked from Carl to Cindy and then to the translator.

"Of course," he said, breaking out with a big smile. "My only intention of course was to introduce our guests to the splendid team of election officers that we have here in Chesterbrook. Having accomplished that task I am most happy to return to the company of the marvelous Democratic poll watchers outside." With that Biff strode from the gym.

Cindy then went through a quick mental list of some of the things she would say to the Brazilians. She realized that Carl could do a more thorough job but it was no more his responsibility than it was Biff's. She did need however to acknowledge his support.

"I guess I should say 'thank you,'" she whispered to Carl. It came out a little less graciously than she intended.

"And I guess I should say 'bite me,' but I won't," replied Carl.

He then turned around and returned to the EPB table.

34

TUESDAY, 10:40 A.M.

To HER SURPRISE Cindy enjoyed her interactions with the Brazilians. She had become knowledgeable enough to be able to give them a more-than-adequate high level explanation of the voting process. Once she got rolling, her charm and skill as a presenter took over. Through their translator (who by now Cindy realized was speaking Portuguese, not Spanish), they asked a number of thought provoking questions that she strived to answer as best she could. By the time she had completed her overview and led them back into the gym, she felt she had regained control of the situation. The Brazilians watched the voting for about ten minutes and took their leave but not before a few of them insisted on having their photos taken with Cindy.

Having said goodbye to the guests she returned to the chief's table where she began reviewing parts of the manual that she still felt a bit shaky on. She was bent over the manual in deep concentration when she heard a voice with which she had become all too familiar.

"Ms. Phelps," said the voice but the tone was altogether different. It sounded, almost pleasant. She looked up and there once again was Biff Logan, this time standing next to a short, somewhat dowdy, gray haired woman who appeared to be in her sixties.

"I would like to introduce you to Emily Weston, the Democratic Party candidate for State Senate. Emily, this is Cynthia Phelps, the chief election officer here at Chesterbrook."

Cindy stood up and greeted the candidate.

"I'm afraid I've been holding a mini-news conference on your lawn," said Emily. "Outside the forty foot line of course. I've been told that I can stay inside for ten minutes and observe things."

"Well I'll be heading outside. I'm sure we'll be seeing each other again Ms. Phelps," said Biff.

"Very good," said Cindy. Then, reflecting that courtesy was indeed a two way street, she added, "Mr. Logan, So far today you have addressed me as Missy, Little Miss Coed, and Ms. Phelps. I think it's time you started calling me Cindy."

Biff flashed a winning smile. "You got it....Cindy." With that he turned and left.

"I gather you've had some dealings with our esteemed Democratic chairman," said Emily.

"You might say that. He can certainly change his approach."

"He's a lawyer."

"Well anyway, you have ten minutes. You can spend it talking to me or you can wander around on your own. Just don't disrupt the process."

"I'm not sure I'd know what to look for. The last thing I ever expected to be is a political candidate."

You and me both, thought Cindy. However she refrained from commenting. She had to remember that Emily was a candidate and it would not do for Cindy to be sharing her lack of experience or insecurities.

They stood together for a couple of minutes. Then Emily said, "I'd best be on my way. I still have three other precincts to visit." They shook hands and Emily departed, stopping briefly on the way out to say a few words to the Democratic poll watchers.

Cindy looked down at her cell. It was 11:00 a.m. The polls had been open for five hours. There were still eight hours to go.

35

TUESDAY, 11:00 A.M.

CINDY PERFORMED HER hourly numbers check and recorded the vote count, 298, into the log. Therefore it did not surprise her when Jerry announced, a couple of minutes later that they were now on their fourth pack of ballots. She then returned to the EPB table and relieved Theodore who had taken her place when she had gone to help the Brazilians.

"We're starting our fourth package of ballots," she said to Carl. "We started with six. Do you thing we're OK?"

He thought for a few seconds. "The turnout is higher than I would have anticipated. But I still think we've got enough."

They sat side by side, each processing voters from the small line that never quite seemed to disappear. In addition to the retired folks, they were beginning to see younger people. Cindy guessed that these were individuals who both lived and worked locally and were voting on their lunch break.

"Kreigson. Michael David Kreigson."

"Very good Mr. Kreigson. May I see your ID please?"

Mr. Kreigson immediately handed over his driver's license. Cindy noticed a slight tremor in his hand. He was a youngish man, perhaps about thirty, with what seemed a pleasant face. Cindy quickly looked at the photo on the license which matched that of Mr. Kreigson. She gave him an encouraging smile. "This will only take a minute Mr. Kreigson."

"I can take you ma'am," said Carl to the woman standing next in line. She shook her head and pointed to Cindy. Carl shrugged and said in a somewhat louder voice, "I can take the next in line."

The woman continued to stand in place, a grim look on her face with her coat wrapped tightly around her. She seemed determined that Cindy, and only Cindy, would check her in. The man behind her very tentatively stepped out of the line and began walking slowly toward Carl. It was apparent that he did not want to be accused of "cutting ahead." The woman continued to stand in place and the man eventually came before Carl to be processed.

In the meantime, Cindy found Mr. Kreigson's name on the EPB.

"May I have your address please, Mr. Kreigson?"

"1910 Waverly Court," stammered Mr. Kreigson who seemed rather ill at ease. Cindy checked the EPB; the address matched. She handed the license back to him, again with a smile, trying to put this obviously highly strung young man at ease.

"Michael David Kreigson, 1910 Waverly Court," she announced in a voice sufficiently loud so that the poll watchers could hear. She moved the mouse on the computer so that arrow was directly over the "Check voter in" box when something caught her eye. It was the "Year of Birth" field on the screen and it read "1938." Obviously she had brought up the wrong record.

Nice catch Cindy, she thought. *The last thing I want to do is check in the wrong person. The person before me is probably "the son" and I've pulled up the record of his father.*

"Just a second Mr. Kreigson. I seem to have pulled up the wrong record. I'll get you processed in a jiffy."

Cindy went back to the search screen. She entered "Kreigson" again but only the one record appeared. It seemed that there were no other Kreigsons registered in the precinct. On a hunch she then used the mouse to slide the on-screen bubble from "precinct" to "all." On the county level there were three Kreigson's; Michael, of course, but the other two were female, "Amanda" and "Anne." Cindy returned the bubble to "precinct" and brought Mr. Kreigson's record back up.

"Carl", she said quietly leaning over. "Can I show you something?"

"I'll be with you in a second," said Carl who in the final stages of checking in a voter. "All right sir, here is your ballot card. If you just step over to the ballot table you will receive your ballot. OK, Cindy, what is it?"

Cindy said nothing but just pointed to the "Year of Birth 1938" on the screen.

"So?" said Carl, confused and a bit annoyed.

Cindy said nothing. She continued to look at Carl.

Gradually he understood. He shifted his eyes to the nervous young man in front of them. He then looked back at Cindy.

Trying to maintain her composure, Cindy addressed the young man. "I'm sorry sir but there seems to be an error in the database. I'm going to have to call the Government Center to clear things up. If you would come back with me to the chief's table—"

"No, it's a mistake," said Mr. Kreigson quickly. With that he spun around and hurried from the gym. Likewise the woman who had been standing next in line also turned around and departed.

"Now what was that all about?" asked Cindy.

"I don't know," said Carl "but you better get that into the Chief's Notes while it's still fresh in your head."

Cindy agreed. It was time to switch jobs again anyway. Theodore was sent back to the scanner; Carl to the ballot table; and Pam and

Jerry to the EPBs. Cindy went over to the chief's table and wrote up the incident in the "Chief's Notes."

Having completed that, she undertook some of her other bureaucratic duties. First was the compensation sheet. All election officers were paid for their day's work, very little to be sure, but it was still something. Cindy wrote her own name and address in the top part of the form under "chief." She then went around to each of the officers and had them fill out their information.

Next was the task of making sure each of the officers had a chance to vote. Cindy had already voted herself. Her apartment was actually located within the Cooper precinct, just a little ways from the school and she had voted absentee.

She approached Theodore at the scanner. "If you'd like to vote now, I can take your place here for a few minutes."

Theodore thanked her and went to stand in the short line in front of the EPBs. Within a few minutes he had completed the voting process and returned to his place at the scanner. Cindy then went to each of the officers in turn. Carl had also voted absentee but Jerry and Pam, each in turn, took advantage of her offer.

Cindy was at the EPB table having just given Pam her ballot card. She refreshed her EPB screen and was about to look up when she heard a familiar voice.

"Millicent Joy LaGrande. I am here to exercise my constitutional prerogative."

She looked up. It was indeed Millicent LaGrande in all her regal splendor.

"Yes," said Millicent. "The prodigal daughter has returned; humbled and penitent. And if that offer is still on the table I would like very much to serve as a p.m. officer."

Cindy was overcome with joy. It was like a weight had been lifted from her shoulders. If there hadn't been a table between them she would have hugged Millicent. As it was she stood up and grasped her by the hand. "Yes, absolutely. We would love to have you back. Let's have you vote first and then we'll get you back in harness." The two women stood there for a few moments, beaming at each other.

36

TUESDAY, NOON

MILLICENT'S RETURN WAS like a breath of fresh air, lifting the spirits of the entire team. She was warmly greeted by each member as she worked her way through the voting process. On a purely functional level it gave them a sixth officer which permitted Cindy to be a little more generous in the time she allowed each of the officers to break for lunch. Then a few minutes later they had another visitor as Milton came through the door.

"I'm starting my second round of precinct visits," he said to Cindy who by this time was seated back at the chief's table.

He looked around the gym.

"It seems like everything is working well. It's a bit less hectic than my last visit," he chuckled.

Milton continued, "I can tell that the school is nervous about security. The assistant principal and one of the male teachers seem to have stationed themselves in the hallway just inside the front door. They are greeting the voters as their 'welcomed guests' but they're keeping a sharp eye, lest any of these guests wander off in an inappropriate direction. Otherwise, everything looks good.

The partisans appear to be respecting the forty foot line. A couple of your signs have fallen down. I put them back up but you might want to have someone check them from time to time."

Cindy nodded.

"How are things in the outside world?" she asked.

"Well the temperature's dropped and the clouds are moving in. They say it's going to start raining in about an hour or two. It will begin as drizzle and then pick up. They're not sure whether it will freeze or not."

"That sounds like fun," said Cindy, thinking of the drive to the Government Center that she would have to make that night.

"Well it hasn't happened yet and they don't always get it right."

"How are things going with the other precincts?"

"It's been a fairly busy morning. One of the EPBs at Seneca Grove conked out about mid-morning and I had to swap in a new one which was the last of my extras. Most of the other precincts are doing fine. Heavy turnout at Manchester. Of course we lost the chief at Hagerman due to a personal situation. The new chief is conscientious."

At this point Milton hesitated. He liked Cindy and was inclined to think that she would keep whatever he said confidential but still he needed to be professional in how much he revealed. So he just repeated "very conscientious," rather than saying, "The guy is driving me crazy. I think he knows what to do fairly well but he has zero confidence so he calls me asking for permission every time he wants to tie his shoes."

"And how's Julia doing?" asked Cindy quietly.

This was different. They both knew Julia. And they both were concerned for her.

Milton gave a sigh. "The precinct is functioning fairly well," he said. "I think she'll be OK."

Then he added, "I wish you were there."

Cindy laughed, "I think Carl would agree with that."

"You guys getting along all right?"

"Now why would you ask that?"

"I noticed a bit of tension the last time I was here. Plus I hear things. I don't always know what they mean but I hear things."

Cindy considered. "I think we're OK," she said. "We've both turned down the volume a bit."

"Glad to hear it," said Milton. "Oh and here's that blank oath sheet you asked for. Now if there is nothing else, I'll be on my way."

"Will we see you again today?"

"I'm not sure," he replied. "We'll see how things go. There are a couple of precincts I'm concerned about but this is not one of them. Call me if there are any bumps in the road."

"Will do. Thanks, Milton."

Milton rose to take his leave. He stopped by the EPB table to exchange a few words with Carl and then left the gym.

In the meantime Cindy signed the oath sheet and took it around to each of the team members for their signature. She then returned to the chief's table. She took stock of her situation.

It was 12:30 p.m. The halfway point. 6 ½ hours down; 6 ½ hours to go. The shadow of Millicent's forced departure had been lifted. The team was back to full strength. And while she and Carl were hardly best buds, they had achieved an equilibrium of civility. For the first time she began to see, very faintly, the light at the end of the tunnel. The idea of life continuing after this day no longer seemed absurd.

Her cell phone rang.

"Cindy, it's Roger Dellman."

"Roger, you old so and so," said Cindy brightly. "It's been too long. What's up?"

"Cindy," said Roger with a tone of severity. "We have a situation."

Oh, shit.

"I'm listening."

"What can you tell me about Michael David Kreigson?"

37

TUESDAY, 12:35 P.M.

A SINKING FEELING GRIPPED Cindy. She reached for the Chief's Notes that she had written, not because she had forgotten the event, but rather just to have something to hold on to.

"Let's see," she began trying be as matter-of-fact as possible. "Mr. Kreigson came in to vote a little over an hour ago. He presented an ID, his driver's license, which looked fine—"

"Did you compare the photo on the license with the person before you?"

"Yes."

"OK. Please continue."

Cindy began to feel like she was on the witness stand.

"Once I checked his license I looked up his name in the EPB. It came up so I asked him for his address. What he said matched with what was on the EPB. Everything matched."

"Did you repeat his name and address out loud for the poll workers?"

"Yes, I did."

"And then what happened?"

"Well that's when I noticed that his birth date on the screen said 1938. Mr. Kreigson however was a much younger man. So I thought I had brought up the wrong record and I tried to see if there were any other Kreigsons in the precinct. When I didn't find any, I began to think that there was a mistake in the database. When I started to talk about that to Mr. Kreigson, he said that there was a mistake and he left."

"And that's it?"

"That's it."

"Did you confirm him in the database?"

"No."

"Did you hand him a ballot card?"

"No."

"Did he vote?"

Cindy had had enough.

"Oh yes, Roger. While we weren't looking, he snuck in through a side window, grabbed a ballot, put it in the scanner, and walked out disguised as a Munchkin. Actually he might have voted twice. I was too busy putting on my makeup to notice. Roger, what's this all about?"

"Can anyone corroborate your version of—?"

"My version? I repeat Roger, what is this all about?"

"I'll tell you in a minute. But in the meantime can anyone corroborate your version?"

"Well Carl can to an extent. He was at the EPB table with me and I showed him the 1938 date on the screen. And of course Mr. Kreigson can corroborate it."

"Mr. Kreigson is dead."

"What?"

"Cindy, does your cell phone connect to the internet?"

"Yes, it does but what has that got to do with—"

"I want you to link to the internet. Bring up Google and enter the words 'Virginia Fraud.' Then click on the first YouTube video that you see. And have Carl watch it too. When you have seen it call me back."

They said their goodbyes and hung up. Cindy walked over to Millicent who was serving as a greeter.

"I sense a quest," declared Millicent.

"Hardly," said Cindy trying to keep her tone light. "I want you to relieve Carl at the ballot table. He'll explain to you what needs to be done. Then send him over to me."

"Thy will be done," said Millicent who then hurried off to the ballot table.

Cindy returned to the chief's table. She linked to the internet and brought up Google. She entered "Virginia Fraud" and pressed the search button. The top entry was "Voter Fraud in the Old Dominion." Beside it was a photograph of an elderly man who she did not recognize. At that point she put the phone down and waited for Carl. After a few minutes he came over, a bit of a frown on his face.

"Roger wants us to watch a video. But first I have to ask you. It's about that man with the 1938 birthday. Roger asked me to recount the whole thing in minute detail. Can you confirm that I did not check him in on the EPB?"

"Sure. I mean, I think so. We could enter his name now and see that he hasn't been confirmed. Of course I suppose someone could have confirmed him and later backed it out—"

"Carl, backing out a voter involves some special process that's not even in the manual. Plus you are looking at the person who couldn't even issue a provisional ballot without practically having a nervous breakdown. Do you really think I could have figured out—?"

"No, of course not." Carl spoke slowly as if trying to bring it back in his mind. "I remember you showed me the 1938 date and you were concerned that you had pulled up the wrong record. You then started to talk to him about it and he left."

"OK," said Cindy, trying hard to be calm. "Let's watch the movie."

"Did you bring the popcorn?"

"I don't think it's that kind of movie."

Cindy clicked on the photo and the video came to life. The photo of the elderly man took center stage.

"This is Michael David Kreigson. Mr. Kreigson lives within the boundary of the Chesterbrook precinct which is voting in today's special election. Or rather he used to live in this precinct. For Mr. Kreigson passed away last April. But no matter, here at Chesterbrook, Mr. Kreigson is alive and well."

Suddenly the image on the screen changed and displayed, to Cindy's horror, a video of herself checking in Mr. Kreigson. There she was with her most radiant smile announcing,

"Michael David Kreigson, 1910 Waverly Court."

The video then switched over to another image of Cindy. It was the portion of her interview with Tracy when she had lost her poise.

"Well—uh—no—what I mean is—" The video then froze on her bewildered face.

"It's time for the citizens of Virginia to take voter fraud seriously. As long as our electoral boards insist on appointing inexperienced and incompetent election officers we will be at the mercy of those who would corrupt the voting process. Voter Fraud. It's everyone's problem."

That was the entire video. They both sat in stunned silence. Slowly Cindy leaned forward and buried her face in her hands. She felt duped, violated, but mostly just plain overwhelmed. For a couple of minutes they remained still. Then at last Cindy lifted her head. When she spoke, her voice was flat and drained of any emotion.

"I need to call Roger. You go back to the EPB table. Roger will probably want to talk to you. Tell him whatever you must."

"Cindy, I'm sorry—," Carl began.

Cindy shook her head and gave a wave of her hand that clearly said, "Go away."

Carl nodded and returned to the EPB table.

Cindy, dialed the Government Center.

"Roger, I've seen the video."

"And?"

"I've already told you what happened."

"It's being claimed that the person impersonating Mr. Kreigson left only after you offered him the ballot card. They claim that they were testing the system and that you were prepared to let him vote."

"Who is 'they'?"

"Some group that calls itself 'Virginians against Fraud' or something like that."

There was silence on both ends of the phone. Finally Roger spoke.

"Cindy, the Electoral Board is very upset over this as you might imagine."

She remained silent.

"Is there anything else you want to add?"

"I've already told you what happened."

"OK, I guess that's it for now."

They said their goodbyes and hung up.

Cindy sat in silence. For the first time she asked herself, *"What's the point? Why am I even trying?"*

38

TUESDAY, 1:00 P.M.

"CARL, I NEED the EPB count."

Cindy's voice sounded detached and indifferent. Like she was just going through the motions, which Carl realized was probably the case.

"Let's see. It's 386."

"Thank you." Cindy wrote something in her log and returned to the chief's table.

She's damaged goods, he thought.

The once steady stream of voters was now reduced to a trickle. This frequently happened shortly after the noon hour. Most of the voters coming in were elderly; folks who required a little more time. This was always something that energized Carl. He found it satisfying to make the extra effort so that these voters were treated with respect and given whatever assistance they needed. For the next half hour, Carl lost himself in these efforts. He was vaguely aware of Jerry announcing around 1:15 that they were now on their fifth (and next to last) pack of ballots.

In the meantime Cindy had returned to the chief's table. For several minutes she just sat there, overcome by a sense of hopeless futility. Earlier her tears had actually helped her focus on how she could improve, on what needed to be done. This time it was different. Some of the things that had happened had been her fault. Others had been out of her control. But none of that mattered any more. She was finished.

She picked up a pen and started doodling absentmindedly on her notepad. All around her were the sights and sounds of the precinct but they seemed irrelevant, not part of her world. She looked down at her doodles,

> Dear Carl,
>   I quit.
> Sincerely,
> Cindy

That would solve her problem, she thought. *I'll give him the note, gather up my things, and go home to some daytime TV. It's what Carl wants. Probably Roger, too. So tempting.*

Still she hesitated. When was the last time she had quit? She remembered dropping a couple of courses in college but that was different. She had dropped those because she wasn't interested. This time she was bailing out because she was failing.

But what was the alternative? Why to continue on of course. To continue and fail. To be removed from her position by whoever Roger reported to or alternatively being reduced to some sort of figurehead with Carl actually in charge.

Is that what it all boiled down to? To quit or to fail? Which was worse? Or was there another alternative?

And gradually that other alternative came into focus.

It was an alternative that came from the inner resilience that was part of Cindy's character; that resilience that allowed her to bounce back from adversity no matter how discouraging things might be or no matter how tempting complete surrender might seem.

That "other" alternative was simply to "hang in there" even when success seemed unlikely. To persevere and strive; to keep on learning and trying and doing. To use her abilities and judgements as best she could for as long she was allowed. And ultimately if she failed, to learn from the experience and hopefully grow as a result.

She looked down at her resignation note.

"Not today," she said as she tore the page in two. "Not today."

39

Tuesday, 1:30 p.m.

I T WAS SHORTLY after 1:30 when Carl's cell phone rang. He had expected this and was actually a bit surprised that it had not happened sooner.

"Carl, this is Roger. We need to have a conversation and you need to be somewhere where you can't be overheard. Can you manage that?"

"I think so, Roger. We're not terribly busy right now. Let me arrange it and I'll call you back."

He crossed over to Cindy.

"Cindy, I'm sorry but something has come up and I need to make a brief personal call. Can you fill in for me at the EPB table?"

Cindy nodded. She actually seemed a bit more focused than she had been just a few minutes earlier. Hopefully that was a good sign.

Carl went into the PE office off the gym which was fortunately vacant. He dialed into the Command Center.

"OK Roger, we can talk."

"Carl, I've been directed by the Electoral Board to ask you the following question." Roger's voice was stiff and formal, almost like he was reading from a script.

"Go on."

"Are you prepared to take over the Chesterbrook precinct?"

"What?"

"Are you prepared to assume the duties as chief of the Chesterbrook precinct?"

"That's a strange question Roger. Anyone who is an assistant chief knows that they could assume those duties if the chief is called away or becomes incapacitated or whatever. Roger, just what is happening?"

"Carl, in a few minutes the board is going into executive session. The item on the agenda is the proposed removal of Cindy Phelps as chief."

Carl couldn't believe what he was hearing.

"Because of the video?"

"Mostly. The board was also displeased by the Tracy Miller interview this morning. In addition a Mr. Carson has called complaining that he was mistreated and shown a lack of respect by Cindy. But mostly it's the video. It's a madhouse over here. The Republicans are threatening to challenge the results no matter what. Biff Logan and the Democrats are threatening to sue. And the State Board is asking questions. They want to know if things are out of control at Chesterbrook and what we are doing to rectify the situation."

"Well for what it's worth, you can discount the whole Mr. Carson thing. The man was not in the pollbook and he went ballistic over it. Cindy remained calm under trying circumstances and did everything by the book. If anyone was mistreated it was her. I agree that she let the Tracy Miller interview go on too long. It was a rookie mistake which I doubt will ever happen again."

"And the video?"

"It's misleading to say the least. Cindy was in the process of checking him in but then she noticed the 1938 'date of birth' which did not correspond to the young man in front of her. She was trying to figure out what to do next when he bolted. She never checked him in or gave him a ballot card."

"They're claiming that she was on the verge of giving out the ballot card and confirming him in the EPB when he voluntarily left. It was a ruse by a group called 'Virginians against Fraud' to test the system. So once again I need to ask, are you prepared to assume the duties as chief of the Chesterbrook precinct?"

Carl's head was spinning. He had expected that they might ask him to give her some counseling but never this. He had never heard of a chief being discharged for making a single mistake. And this wasn't even a mistake. What he needed was some time to think.

"Roger, this is quite a surprise as you can imagine. Can I have a little time to think it over?"

"I can give you maybe a minute or two but that's it. They're about to go into executive session."

They hung up and Carl tried to come to grips with the situation. He was the type of person who tried to look at things from all sides before making up his mind.

One side was obvious. This was simply not fair. Cindy might not be his favorite chief or even his favorite person but she didn't deserve this. That video was a manufactured piece of nonsense. The idea of self-appointed interest groups creating artificial hoops for election officers to jump through was repulsive to him. Such sensationalism also lessened the likelihood of any serious discussion of voter fraud which in Carl's mind was a very legitimate concern.

On the other hand, he was absolutely certain that he could do a far better job as election chief than Cindy. Her less than stellar preparation, her inexperience, and even at times her temperament had all contributed to making this a more difficult day than it should have been. Carl was not blind to her strengths. She was intelligent and could be very personable. She also had a tenacity and toughness which, up until now at least, had allowed her to bounce back from adversity. With time and experience she would become a good chief but she wasn't there yet.

In addition Carl had to think of his own position. Simply put, Carl loved being an election officer. He loved the whole concept of seven or eight people from different walks of life and different political persuasions gathering together at 5:00 a.m. and then working closely together for the next fifteen hours to do something worthwhile. It was an experience that truly added richness to his life. He had to ask himself if defying the Electoral Board at this time would jeopardize his being able to serve in the future. Did he really want to risk all that defending a person who he did not particularly like and who in all probability despised him?

His phone rang.

"Carl, the session is about to begin. Are you prepared to assume the duties as chief of the Chesterbrook precinct?"

That was it. The time for analysis was over. A decision was required, and it was required now. And it was at that moment that Carl realized that this whole situation wasn't so much about Cindy's qualities as a chief as it was about his substance as a person. And with that understanding, all thoughts of videos and elections faded

from his mind. And fading away as well was the ambiguity and un-
certainty leaving only the obvious answer that had to be given.

"No."

"Carl, do realize what—"

"No Roger, let me finish. If Cindy is removed as chief I will not
take her place. Moreover I will not continue to serve as assistant
chief or even election officer for that matter under any chief other
than Cindy. Since when does the Board get rid of someone for a
single mistake? You knew she was inexperienced when you selected
her. And this wasn't even a mistake."

"That video is bogus and you know it. The only fraud that has
been committed this day was by the people who made it. Cindy has
done her job and continues to do her job 'according to law and the
best of her ability.' Now it is time for the board to do its job and
publically denounce that video as the piece of trash that it is."

Then as afterthought Carl added, "And Roger, you may also
tell the board that I know a thing or two about making videos and
if they throw Cindy under the bus, there will be within the hour,
another video on YouTube that will tell to whoever might be interested, exactly what has transpired this day."

For a few seconds, the air hung heavy with Carl's declaration.

At last Roger said, "I will pass your sentiments on to the board."

"Thank you. I would appreciate that."

"So, how are things going over there?"

"Couldn't be better, Roger. Couldn't be better."

40

TUESDAY, 1:50 P.M.

CARL COULDN'T HELP it. He felt good. There is a certain liberating feeling that comes from having to make a tough decision and choosing the "right" over the "tempting" or the "easy." How it would play out was anyone's guess. By his own words he had dictated that if Cindy was let go, he would leave as well. Carl wondered who would take over in that case. Pam was probably the most qualified. She had been offered a chief's position a number of times in the past, but had always declined. Perhaps under these circumstances she would accept. Or they might bring Milton in. Well, whatever it was, it would happen soon. In the meantime it was back to work.

He returned to the EPB table. On his way back, he couldn't resist a chuckle. That last minute add-on had been a complete bluff. He didn't know the first thing about creating videos.

"I can take over here," he said to Cindy. "You should probably prepare for the 2:00 p.m. call in."

She gave him a questioning look. She seemed to sense that Carl's call had involved her. He tried to give her a reassuring smile. Without a word she got to her feet and returned to the chief's table.

They had reached the low ebb of the day in terms of voters. Every couple of minutes a voter or two would come in but that was it. Carl couldn't help but notice that for the first time some of these voters were sporting raincoats.

"Your count please, Carl?"

It was Cindy. She seemed more upbeat than before. She had a look about her, almost as if she had decided to do something.

"We are at 438," was his reply.

"Plus the three over there marking their ballots makes 441. Thanks, Carl."

"Base to all precincts. It's time for the 2:00 p.m. call in. Let us have your vote totals please."

"Base, Easthampton once again is first to report with 432 voters."

"Copy that, Easthampton."

Carl was glad that Cindy had already determined her number. At least she would not be among the last to check in. Any little thing that helped dispel the notion that Chesterbrook was "out of control" as Roger had suggested, wouldn't hurt.

"Base, Wallingford stands at 412."

"Copy that, Wallingford. Thanks."

"Base, this is Danby and we have 401."

"Copy that, Danby. Great to hear from you."

What was Cindy waiting for? She had her number. Why didn't she call it in?

"Base, Seneca Grove is checking in with 398."

"Copy that, Seneca Grove."

Carl looked over at the chief's table. She was just sitting there. The radio was on the table. This was ridiculous. He got up and walked quickly toward the table.

"Base, this is Manchester; the biggest and the best leads all the rest with 612 voters."

"Copy that, Manchester. You're an inspiration to us all."

"Cindy, you need to call in your number now," said Carl.

"Not yet," she said.

"What do you mean not yet? It's the two o'clock call. What are you waiting for?"

"We're waiting on Hagerman, Chesterbrook and Cooper. We need your numbers."

The now familiar high pitched voice came over the radio.

"Base, Hagerman is reporting 407 voters."

"Copy that, Hagerman. Keep up the good work. We need Chesterbrook and Cooper."

"Cindy, you need to—"

Cindy gave Carl a stern look and raised her hand in a gesture that clearly meant "be quiet."

"We need numbers from Chesterbrook and Cooper."

The seconds ticked by. Carl was incredulous.

"Chesterbrook and Cooper. You need to check in!"

Then at last,

"Base, this is the Cooper precinct. We have a number…let me see…our number is…is…431."

"Copy that, Cooper. Chesterbrook. Where are you? We need your numbers."

At last Cindy picked up her radio. She pressed the button and in a calm, crystal clear voice she reported in,

"Base, Chesterbrook is bringing up the rear in style with 441 voters."

"Copy that, Chesterbrook. Glad you're among the living. Thank you all precincts for your numbers. The next call in will come at the end of the day when you radio in your final results. Keep up the good work everyone."

Cindy put down the radio and turned to face Carl, "I'm sorry but I just didn't want Julia to be the last one."

He started to say something but she held up her hand again for silence. Then speaking calmly as one who was at peace with her situation she said,

"Carl, if they want me gone then I'm gone and being first with the numbers isn't going to save my ass. But for now, I'm still the chief and you still are not, so what you need to do is get back to your EPB station, and you will do your job and I will do my job and we'll just see how this whole thing plays out."

41

TUESDAY, 2:20 P.M.

"*A*TTENTION ALL STUDENTS. *Attention all students. The local weather channel is predicting possible freezing rain for later this afternoon so all after-school activities have been cancelled. I repeat, all after-school activities have been cancelled.*"

"So what time does school get out?" asked Cindy who had repositioned herself at the EPB table.

"School ends at 3:05 on the dot," said Carl. "Mrs. Martin will come in and ask me—I mean, ask you—if you need anything and that will be it. With after-school activities canceled, the school will be a ghost town by 3:30."

"Except for us."

"Except for us and the p.m. custodian who I will add, I have never seen in the five years I've served here. I've been assured that he exists and I've tried locating him once or twice but to no avail."

At that point five voters walked in. They appeared to be unrelated and formed an orderly queue.

Carl's first voter was a woman who immediately presented her driver's license.

"Fiona Montanez."

He located her entry in the EPB.

And your address ma'am.

"432 Van Buren Street."

Carl looked at the address in the EPB. It did not agree with what the woman had stated.

"Your registration is listed at 9001 Jackson Street, ma'am."

"Oh, I moved from there long ago."

"How long?"

"Let's see, it was when the kids were still at home. I don't know. Ten years? Twelve years?"

Carl was amazed that the woman had apparently been voting for years and years, registered at the wrong address.

"Have you been voting all this time and not reporting your address change to us? I assure you it's very easy to fill out the form."

"Oh no. I haven't been voting. I'm only here because my grandson goes to school with one of Jennifer's Haley's kids. So he said I need to vote for her." She showed him a Haley bumper sticker.

"The problem is ma'am that you moved so long ago. If you had moved since last November's election to anywhere else in Virginia you can return to your old precinct and vote. If you moved before then it gets more complicated. If you moved sometime before last November's election but since the last presidential election then you may return to your old precinct if, and here it gets tricky, you stayed within the same county and the same congressional district."

Carl flashed a big smile after his legalistic pronouncement. He was proud of having memorized it by heart. "I'm afraid that since you moved well before the last presidential election you are out of luck. But if you fill out a voter registration form we can get you all set up for the next election."

"So how do I fill out this form?" Ms. Montanez asked.

"Carl, she's in the same precinct, isn't she?" interjected Cindy, who was processing her own voter but apparently had overheard part of Carl's declaration.

"If you follow me over to the chief's table, I'll give you the form," said Carl to the woman. "You can fill it out right now."

He stood up and led the lady over to the chief's table and showed her how to fill out the form. He then returned to the EPB table. "Next person, please," he said motioning to the next person in line.

"Carl, that woman you were just dealing with. She moved within the precinct, didn't she?" asked Cindy who had just given a ballot card to her voter.

"Your full name please," Carl was asking the man who had been next in line.

"Carl—"

"What is it Cindy?" said Carl who was rather annoyed in having his flow interrupted. He was rather proud of the efficient way that he processed voters at the EPB table.

"That last woman. She moved within the precinct."

"So?"

"So she can vote."

"Let me explain, Cindy," said Carl who continued to be annoyed. "If you moved sometime before the last November election but since the last presidential election then you may return—"

Before he could finish, Cindy got up and went back to the chief's table. Carl could hear her say, "Don't go anywhere" to Ms. Montanez. She then returned with the manual.

"Cindy," said Carl. "We have a line."

"Screw the line," said Cindy, leafing through the manual. "I know it's in here somewhere."

Carl was exasperated. The passage in the manual was complicated but not that complicated. Perhaps if he just explained more slowly, she would understand, "Please, let me explain it to you one more time. If you moved sometime before the last November election but since the last presidential election then you may return—"

"Here," she boldly proclaimed. "Carl, look right here. She can vote."

He looked at the page. His face dropped. Of course. If you're in the same precinct, it didn't matter when you moved. You could go back as long as that precinct had been in existence. How had he missed it?

Cindy couldn't resist, "You really should read the manual, Carl. It's got a lot of good stuff."

Carl was devastated. The minute Cindy had shown him the page, he knew he had been wrong. And of course he was very well acquainted with that section of the manual. He had just been so wound up in the minutiae of the previous entry that his mind had slid past it.

He looked up. She was back at the chief's table talking to Ms. Montanez. "Ma 'am, we are terribly sorry. You certainly may vote. Once you finish filling out the form, come back to the check-in table and come to the front of the line."

Cindy then returned to the EPB table. "I'm sorry for the delay," she said to the voter she had been processing. "Now where were we?"

Carl leaned over, "Cindy, I'm sorry."

"Not now Carl. We have a line."

For the next few minutes the two of them worked side by side processing the small line of voters. Ms. Montanez returned from the chief's table with her registration form filled out. Carl was open at the time and he motioned for her to come forward but she shook her head.

"I will wait for her," she said, pointing at Cindy who was just finishing with another voter.

The two continued processing the small line of voters. Within a few minutes the line was gone.

"You enjoyed that, didn't you," said Carl. He said it like a statement of fact, not an accusation.

"Yes I did, rather," said Cindy brightly.

"I can't believe I missed that. It's such a basic thing."

"Yes, Carl. You screwed up. For the first time in your election career you screwed up."

"The first time? Not hardly."

Cindy was intrigued but said nothing.

"The first time I was chief was at a different precinct. We were using touch screen machines at the time. The only printed ballots were for handicapped people voting curbside. We were given specific instructions to maintain control over those ballots so I kept them with me at all times."

"Anyway I needed to call the Command Center to ascertain the status of some voters. This was before I had a cell phone, so I made my call from the teacher's lounge and I failed to tell my assistant chief that I had the ballots. When I made the call I was placed on hold for about twenty minutes. During that time a handicapped person requested curbside assistance. The assistant chief searched high and low for the ballots but of course couldn't find them. The person was on the verge of giving up and not voting when I returned to the gym."

"Wow," said Cindy softly. "I bet the assistant gave you holy hell over that."

"No, she didn't. She had been chief at that precinct before, but this was another one of those times when the party in power changed so I was named in her place. She was very supportive though. A lot more supportive than I've been of you."

He hadn't really meant to say that last bit. It just sort of came out and caught them both by surprise. They stared at each other. It was like they were looking at each other for the first time.

Carl broke the silence. "I cannot believe with all my experience that I messed it up just now."

"You would have called the Command Center before sending the woman away and they would have cleared it up."

"How do you know that?"

"Because it's just the sort of thing you would do."

"Perhaps. But I still can't believe that I—"

"Carl, stop it," snapped Cindy. "You made a mistake. Welcome to the club. Do you want to keep score? Let's see, where should I begin? I neglected to call the school before the holidays like I should have. And I was too busy partying to contact my officers until the last minute. And I never checked my supplies; now that was a winner; remember all the fun we had with the oath sheet. And I kept forgetting things like the kit and ballot cards. Then I botched up the Tracy Miller interview. Plus I couldn't even process a provisional ballot without going off the rails and don't forget I came within the whisker of letting the fake Mr. Kreigson vote."

"And probably worst of all," continued Cindy, who suddenly found herself unable to look at Carl in the eye, "were the times when I allowed my petty little turf war with you get in the way of what really needed to be done."

"Carl, I'm not exactly sure why, but it appears that they are not going to fire me. So we still have over four hours to go followed by the closing. That's ample time for me to royally screw up this election, so as endearing as your new found humility might be, what we really need is for you to go back to being the know-it-all prick that you and I both know is the real you."

Now it was Cindy's turn to be shocked by her own words. "Wow, I can't believe I just said that."

For the first time in their brief acquaintance, Carl laughed out load. "You certainly know how to make someone feel appreciated."

You should laugh more often, thought Cindy. *It makes you look a whole lot better.*

"As do you sir," she replied as three new voters entered the gym. "Break's over. Let's nail this thing."

42

TUESDAY, 3:05 P.M.

"CARL, DO YOU need anything?" Mrs. Martin was standing in the doorway of the gym, already in her raincoat.

"You have to ask Cindy," called Carl from the EPB table even as Cindy got up and crossed over to the doorway.

"I think we're fine Mrs. Martin," she said. "Everything will be either taken away by us tonight or put back in the precinct cart."

"Very good. The office will be open for about twenty minutes more if you need anything," said Mrs. Martin.

"How is it outside?"

"Right now it's sort of a chilly mist. But the rain should start to intensify in an hour or so."

"I pity the poor party poll workers out there."

"Don't. Most of them have left."

"Interesting," said Cindy. "The poll watchers here inside left about fifteen minutes ago. They said they would return for the close."

"Well, I'll be off," said Mrs. Martin. "Good luck with all your travels this evening."

As Mrs. Martin was leaving, a young man entered the gym. He appeared to be in his early twenties, wore glasses, and had a rather earnest look about him.

"Excuse me, I'm one of the party volunteers outside. There is a bus from the senior center parked in the side parking lot. The bus driver indicated that they want to vote curbside."

"Thank you. We'll take care of it," said Cindy. The young man turned around and left the gym.

Cindy stood at the chief's table trying to decide the best way to proceed. Carl approached her.

"It's the senior center bus isn't it? This is really a two person job. One person takes the lead inside the bus. The other is the 'gofer' who takes things back and forth between the bus and the EPB and/or the scanner. There is no single right way to do this but there are plenty of wrong ways. I would like to take the lead on this."

When she did not immediately answer, he added, "Please."

"All right, Carl. I'll go with you," replied Cindy, a bit intrigued on how he was going to pull this off. She then called over to Pam, "Carl and I are handling the senior citizen bus. Take Carl's place at the check-in table. And send someone out to get me if I'm needed."

"All we will need for the first go round are a couple of clip-boards, each with a piece of paper," said Carl.

They then proceeded out the side door of the gym.

"Just to warn you. This is going to take a bit of time," he said.

"Fortunately, my schedule is free."

"Good. Step one. I will take one side of the bus and you take the other. Collect their photo IDs and ask them their current address. If it is different from what's on the ID, write it down. You then go inside and check them in on the EPB."

They reached the bus; Carl gave a knock on the door; and the bus driver let them in.

"Good afternoon," Carl called out to the residents in a cheerful voice that Cindy had rarely seen him use. "I am Carl Marsden, assistant chief here at the Chesterbrook precinct and this is Cindy Phelps, chief election officer and we are going to help you vote in this special election. Our first step is to collect your photo IDs. Please have them available as we come down the aisle."

It was slow going. Some of the residents had their IDs readily available but others had to hunt through their wallets and handbags. All claimed as their current address the senior citizen home. Two of the residents said they were not interested in voting but had just come along for the ride.

Once all the IDs had been collected, Carl gave Cindy the ones he had. They had fifteen altogether.

"Take these inside and confirm them on the EPB. Then bring fifteen ballots out with the privacy folders, clipboards, and some pens. Also bring some *Request for Assistance* forms. I'll think we'll need a fair number."

Cindy returned to the gym and started to confirm each of the senior citizens. For each ID, she entered the name, checked the address, and then spoke the name and address in an audible voice as the law required. Fortunately all the people were in the EPB. They would not have to turn anyone away. She then gathered up the necessary ballots and clipboards. She put them all in a couple of canvas bags taken from the cart. It was time consuming.

Returning to the bus, she noticed that the cold mist seemed to have become a drizzle. There was a definite chill in the air but for now it seemed to be above freezing. She regretted having left her coat in the car.

As she got back on the bus, Cindy noted a rather festive mood in the air.

"Our leader has returned with the ballots," called out Carl. "Let's hear it for her."

A cheer went up from the residents.

Next Carl explained the drill. "Now we're going to give you back your ID along with your ballot. Each of you will receive a ballot, folder, clipboard, and pen. There is only one contest which is for State Senate. Be sure to fill in the oval for your selection in its entirety. When you are finished, put the ballot back in the folder and raise your hand. If you need help in marking your ballot, just hold on to it. We will help you."

Then Carl turned to Cindy. "This is important; when you start to collect the completed ballots make a note of who the voter is. That way, if the scanner rejects the ballot, we will know which person to return it to."

The two of them started calling out names and handing the residents their IDs and ballots. The first woman that Cindy handed a ballot to immediately complained.

"Why, I don't know who these people are. How am I supposed to choose?"

"It's not my place to tell you," said Cindy. "It's your choice to make."

"Well I suppose I want the Republican. My late husband always said 'vote Republican.'"

"Well, one of the candidates has an 'R' next to his name; the other has a 'D.' Perhaps that might help," said Cindy hoping that she wasn't crossing the line.

"Here, why don't you scan these," said Carl, handing Cindy four folders.

She walked back into the gym. Three of them scanned fine. One rejected with a message that indicated that there were stray marks on the ballot. She obtained a replacement ballot and made a hash mark on the spoiled ballot envelope. She then took the ballot that had failed, wrote "spoiled" on it and put it in the envelope.

Returning to the bus, she gave the new ballot to Carl. "Mrs. Davis' ballot rejected. Here's a fresh one; we will probably have to help her."

And so it continued. "Well thank you. You're a real dear to be doing this," said one lady to Cindy. "I don't see very well you know."

The woman was able to sign her name on the assistance form however and Cindy then explained the ballot.

"Oh I like the Democrat," the woman said. "Please mark it down," which Cindy did. A few rows down she could hear Carl saying,

"Mr. Borden. It is so nice to see you again. I hope your daughter is well."

"Oh yes. She couldn't bring me today so I'm taking the bus," replied Mr. Borden in a hoarse whisper. "But you don't need to help me. I know who I want."

"Of course, Mr. Borden. You tell your daughter hello from me."

"I certainly will young man."

Cindy and Carl worked on. Of the fifteen residents, only six were able to vote unaided. The rest required special assistance. Every time a couple of residents completed their ballot, Cindy would take them in to be scanned. Two more failed to scan and replacement ballots were issued. It was a slow grind. Cindy soon tired of repeating the same instructions over and over again. She couldn't help but notice that Carl never rushed a voter; never showed the least bit of impatience.

At last they were done. Cindy was exhausted. *This really is a long day*, she thought.

"We'll see you all in November," called out Carl. They left the bus to a final round of cheers from the residents.

They came back into the gym. It was a little past 4:00 p.m. It had taken a full hour to process the senior bus. Voters were trickling in, a few at a time, all in raingear. Cindy was drained but there really wasn't any way to take a break. Pam and Theodore had been working the EPBs for the past hour and Theodore, who was tiring rapidly, needed a break. Millicent seemed to be doing all right on the scanner and Jerry was in his element at the ballot table.

"Theodore, you can take a break. Carl why don't you work the EPBs with Pam," she said. "I'm going back to the chief's table and start organizing the forms and envelopes for the close."

When she got back to the chief's table, Cindy began by spreading out the different large envelopes in numerical order. Each one would be filled at the end of the day with the various forms and documents from the day's activities.

She had been going over the various items for a few minutes when she realized that Carl had come back.

"Just a very few voters right now. It should pick up in an hour but for now Pam has got it covered. Would you like me to help you organize this stuff?"

Cindy nodded and for the next few minutes they worked together organizing the materials.

"You were really good with those seniors," she observed. "I must confess that after a while my patience grew thin."

"It's always been one of my favorite parts of being an election officer," said Carl, "Those people have been voting for fifty, sixty, for some even seventy years. They've kept it going. Now it's our turn."

"Our turn to do what?"

"Why to keep the system going, of course. For over two hundred years our electoral system has been the model for the world. Do you know what John Adams, John Quincy Adams, Martin Van Buren, Grover Cleveland, Benjamin Harrison, William Howard Taft, Herbert Hoover, Jimmy Carter and George Herbert Walker Bush all have in common?"

"They were ...uh...all presidents?" asked Cindy. Actually she wasn't sure about a couple of them. History had never been her favorite subject. She also had the feeling that she was about to hear a monologue, one that Carl had given before.

"They were all presidents who were voted out of office. And they all left...peacefully. Just imagine; the year was 1800. The Czars will still running things in Russia; mad King George was on the throne in England; and France was less than a decade removed from the Reign of Terror. While in the United States, President John Adams, who vehemently opposed many of the things his opponent stood for, voluntarily surrendered power just because of what happened in an election."

"Of course it was a bit different then from the elections we have today. In the beginning it was only white property holding males who could vote. But the principle of free elections had been established. It's been passed down through the generations with each one striving to keep it going and improve it whenever they could."

"And today just think of it; on Election Day untold thousands of ordinary Americans put their personal lives and political persuasions on hold to ensure that our elections are run fairly and according to law. We have been referred to as 'the Gatekeepers of Democracy.' What a privilege that is. And if you don't think it's special, take a look at the evening news and see how they do it in other parts of the world."

Cindy really couldn't think of anything to add so she kept silent. Twelve hours earlier, she would have been screaming "Enough already with the history lesson!" But having worked the better part of a day with Carl, she had come to appreciate his passion for election service, a passion that she could respect even if not yet fully embrace. She was now at least beginning to realize that there was more to this than just his quirky little hobby or her need to have "community service" checked off.

The two continued to work quietly together, when Jerry called over to them.

"Just to let you know Cindy. We're now beginning our last pack of one hundred."

"Thank you, Jerry," said Cindy.

Carl said nothing but grabbed a blank sheet of paper and started writing numbers. He then looked up at Cindy with an alarmed expression on his face.

"What is it Carl?" she asked.

"We're going to run out of ballots."

43

TUESDAY, 4:15 P.M.

"THE MATH IS actually quite simple." Carl explained. "We have been open for ten hours and so far have used five hundred ballots. That's an average of fifty ballots per hour. At that rate we will run out somewhere in the 6:00 p.m. range."

"But don't those five hundred ballots include the first few hours when we had the most voters?" asked Cindy.

"True," agreed Carl. "But it also includes the last three hours when turnout was quite light. Look this isn't an exact science especially since this is a 'special' election. But there has been a lot of publicity so it wouldn't surprise me to see a heavy turnout in the last two hours."

"I'll call Milton. They said at that meeting that he would have extras." With that Cindy placed her call.

"Hello Cindy. How is everything going?"

"It's been an interesting day, Milton. We've just opened our last pack of ballots and Carl's done some quick calculations. He doesn't think they will last until 7:00 p.m. Do you have some more that we can have?"

"I'm afraid not. I gave my last batch to Manchester about thirty minutes ago."

"Can you get more from the Government Center?"

"Again, I'm afraid not. They gave me all their extras. You can try calling them but I don't think they can print them fast enough to do you any good. Why don't you plan on having the voters use the 'Create Ballot' machine to produce their ballot, just like it does for the handicapped voters?"

"That's a negative, Milton. Remember both our machines failed."

"Oh yes, that's right. Well it looks like you might have to use the copier in the school office to make copies. They might not scan of course, but the voters can put them in the auxiliary slot to be hand counted. But remember that you need to call the Government Center to get permission."

"OK, I'll get on it. Will we see you again today?"

"Not unless you need to. I've been pretty busy this afternoon, rebooting EPBs and the like. And I remain concerned about my two favorite precincts. So I'll wish you good luck."

"Thanks, Milton. Bye."

Cindy turned to Carl. "Milton has no more ballots. We will need to reproduce them on the school copier."

"But the copier is in the office and I'm sure they locked the door when they left."

"Well that means you will have to locate your invisible friend, the p.m. custodian, to unlock the door," said Cindy with a grim smile. "While you do that, I'll call the Government Center and get permission to make—Don't look at me like that Carl! There are only so many rooms in the school. He has to be in one of them."

"Cindy, you don't understand. I have looked for him before and I tell you—"

"I'm not listening. Try every door of every room. Ground level and second level. Don't forget the bathrooms. Also try the area in the back by the dumpster. There are a couple of doors out there. Probably the boiler room or something."

"How do you know what's out by the dumpster?"

"I'm a smart girl. I know things," said Cindy turning around to look at the EPB table. A line of six voters had queued up in front of Pam. "In the meantime, get going Carl. They're coming to gobble up our ballots."

44

TUESDAY, 4:25 P.M.

CARL BEGAN HIS quest by going down the long hallway that separated the gym from the rest of the school. He regarded this
as being a rather futile effort but realized that it had to be undertaken. Upon reaching the main hallway he gazed upon the office
door with its glass window. On the other side of the door was the
coveted copying machine. He tried the door handle. Locked as
expected.

He then proceeded down the main hall trying the doors of
each of the classrooms. They were all locked. The bathrooms were
unlocked but proved empty of inhabitants. The library door was
open but once again its interior was void of humanity.

"Is anybody there?" he shouted. "I'm looking for the custodian."

Nothing. His voice seemed to echo down the hall. At the end of
the hallway was a staircase. He really didn't expect the custodian to
hang out on the second floor but he went up the stairs anyway. He
repeated the same drill on the second floor with the same result.
Anything that looked like a door was tested. "Is anybody here?" he
shouted multiple times.

Back to the ground level he went. There was still the cafeteria to search and the cooking area. Again nothing. Then he saw the door to the back of the building. This must lead to the area that Cindy had described. He opened the door and walked out.

His feet immediately gave way from under him. He pitched forward toward the concrete but reflexively reached forward and his hands absorbed the worst of the fall. The palms of his hands were scraped and he was a bit shaken but otherwise unhurt. He allowed himself a few moments to regain his composure and then slowly got up, taking stock of his surroundings. It was obvious why he had lost his balance.

The entire area had frozen over. Black ice. That misty drizzle was beginning to freeze over, especially in areas like this with virtually no human traffic to warm the concrete.

He saw the two doors that Cindy had referred to. Taking very short steps he proceeded over to where they were. He tried each of the door handles but they were locked. He knocked and then pounded on each of the doors.

"Is anybody there?" he shouted. There was no reply. Gradually he worked his way back over to the door of the school and reentered the building.

He had searched everywhere he could think of and he had failed. Walking back to the gym, he tried to think of an alternative plan. It was time to think outside the box. Way outside.

45

"**A**RE YOU SURE you searched everywhere?" repeated Cindy, incredulous that the custodian was nowhere to be found.

"Everywhere," said Carl. It was an odd feeling. For the first time today it was Cindy who was disappointed with Carl's performance and not the other way around.

"Well we need to think of something and we need to think fast," said Cindy who then called over to Jerry, "How many ballots do we have left?"

Jerry had interlaced the remaining ballots into groups of ten. He counted quickly and called out "sixty-eight."

"And counting those three in the check-in queue," said Cindy, looking over at the EPB table, "means we're down to sixty-five and it's not even five o'clock, yet."

"I do have an idea," said Carl. "It's a bit unorthodox but—"

"I can live with unorthodox," replied Cindy who was thinking, *if it's coming from you Carl, it can't be too unorthodox.*

"It's that strip shopping center about three miles down Carter Street. It's actually a two tiered center. When you pull in off Carter, you are facing the top tier. But if you walk down the stairs on the far end there's a whole row of stores facing the exit off Madison Lane."

"I never shop there but I think I know what you mean."

"Well there is a Staples in that lower tier of stores."

"Are you suggesting—"

"I'll take one of our ballots and drive down there and get a hundred or so copies. I can get there and back in under fifteen minutes."

"It might work," said Cindy thoughtfully. "Only one problem."

"Which is?"

"I'd have to fire you when you got back. Remember Millicent?"

"Come on, Cindy. That's crazy."

"Of course it's crazy. This whole friggin rule driven system is crazy. But it's the alternate reality we have to live with."

They stood in silence for a few minutes, each trying to formulate a plan. Finally Cindy broke the silence.

"I'll get the ballots," she declared. "Carl, you're too valuable to lose. The same goes for Pam and Jerry. I don't think Theodore is up to it and I refuse to fire Millicent twice in one day. That leaves me. And that works. I'm the chief. I'm impervious. I can't fire myself."

"You could always resign."

Cindy broke into a bright smile. "I bet you've been waiting all day to suggest that. Not a chance."

She went over to Jerry. "I've been given permission to make some copies of the ballots. I'll be taking one of these to make the copies."

Jerry gave her one of the ballots in a privacy folder and she went back to Carl. Together they walked to the side door. Carl wasn't sure he followed all her logic but it was obvious that she was determined.

"I should be back in a jiffy. You're in charge while I'm gone." Then with a playful grin, "Do you think you can handle it?"

"I can only try."

"Atta boy."

And with that Cindy opened the door and departed into the darkening evening.

46

TUESDAY, 4:55 P.M.

CINDY WAS GREETED by a cold drizzle as she started down the sidewalk. She could see the frost forming on the grass but so far the pedestrian traffic seemed to have kept the sidewalk free from ice. Out of the corner of her eye she saw one remaining poll worker over by the tree, the same young man who had given them the heads-up about the senior bus.

As she walked down the sidewalk toward the parking lot she passed three different voters coming up toward the school. This impressed upon her the need to make this trip as brief as possible. Reaching the parking lot, she noted a number of puddles that had formed. Some of them were covered by a thin veil of ice. Walking around the puddles she headed to her car at the far end of the lot. This part of the lot had been less used during the day and the pavement under her feet was a bit slippery. Nothing she couldn't handle but she had to slow down a bit from her brisk walk.

Finally she reached her car. Once inside she started the engine and turned on the headlights. The clock on the dash showed the time as exactly 5:00 p.m.

She backed her car out of its parking space, drove over to the exit, and making a right turn pulled into traffic. Although she could see icicles beginning to form on the overhead trees, the traction on the road was good. The street immediately ahead of her was clear but about fifty yards down the road was a car with its brake lights on.

As she approached the car, it became apparent that it was stopped behind a whole line of stationary vehicles. "Damn," she said softly.

For several minutes the line of cars remained at a standstill. The minutes ticked by on the dashboard clock. Just as Cindy was considering a U-turn, the line of cars started to move, slowly at first, and then gradually up to full speed. Eventually she passed a tow truck by the side of the road with its driver tending to a broken down vehicle. Cindy was on the move again but the lost time had been painful. She looked at the clock which read 5:12 p.m.

By the time the shopping center parking lot came into view, Cindy had worked herself into a rather agitated state. She needed to get those ballots reproduced as soon as possible. She also had a distinct feeling that travel conditions were going to deteriorate rather quickly.

She pulled onto the ramp that lead down into the parking lot. Driving down the ramp she saw that the parking lot was practically empty. She also saw the staircase that Carl had referred to at the far end. She needed to get there as quickly as possible. She stepped on the gas, a little too hard, and her car started to go into a spin. With the lot empty she made a quick decision just to let the spin take its course. The car eventually came to a stop but not as quickly as she would have thought. The slippery pavement had prolonged the skid. That should have served as a warning.

Once the car had come to a complete stop, Cindy stepped on the gas, a lighter touch this time, and she guided the car into the parking place closest to the staircase. She looked at the clock. It read 5:15 p.m. Damn, this was taking too long. She grabbed the folder with the ballot and then looked over at her winter coat and boots that had been in the car since morning.

No time for that, she thought. Exiting the car she started to walk toward the staircase. The discomfort of the cold drizzle along with her need to get the job done as quickly as possible caused her to walk quickly and then break into a half trot. She reached the staircase and began to descend the stairs as fast as she could. That was a mistake.

The stairs had not been used for a number of hours and patches of the same black ice that Carl had encountered had begun to form on some of the individual steps. But Cindy wasn't focused on that. Rather she was determined to get down the stairs as quickly as possible. Her feet skipped from step to step, faster and faster, until they came into contact with a patch of slick ice around ten steps from the bottom. Suddenly they gave out from under her, her momentum causing her to lurch forward.

Desperately she reached for the railing with her left hand. She briefly grabbed on but the forward pull of her body caused her wrist to snap back and her grip was lost. A bolt of pain shot from her wrist up her arm. With nothing left to restrain her, she fell forward slamming into the side of the cement staircase with a sickening thud, the left side of her face and body absorbing most of the blow. Emitting an involuntary gasp, she ricocheted off the side and toppled head over heels down the remaining steps landing head-first onto the concrete slab at the bottom of the stairs.

Then ever so slowly she rolled over onto her side curling up into a ball on the muddy ground adjacent to the walkway.

"Oh my God," she moaned in pain. "Oh my merciful God."

47

TUESDAY, 5:20 P.M.

"**P**AM, I THINK I have a workaround with the ballots," said Carl, joining Pam at the EPB table. "I've been playing around with the 'Create Ballot' machine and I can get it to work sometimes."

"Here's your ballot card," said Pam handing the card to the woman she had just checked in. Then turning to Carl. "I thought the machine just returned a blank card when you tried to use it."

"Well sometimes yes. Sometimes no. I've been playing with it and every third time or so it returns a card with the selections marked."

Carl showed some cards he had just created. "I have to destroy these of course. And it returns blank cards much of the time but at least it's something in case we run out before Cindy gets back."

Then calling back to Jerry, "How many ballots do we have now Jerry?"

Jerry had just given the most recent voter her ballot. "We have forty-one left."

By this time six more people had entered the gym. One was a mother with two young children. The children immediately started running around the gym. Theodore attempted to interest them with "I Voted" stickers even as Carl and Pam commenced checking in the voters.

For Carl, every new voter had become part of a mathematical equation. With these four voters they would be down to thirty-seven ballots. He estimated that those remaining ballots would probably get them to the six o'clock time frame but that was it. And then what? That workaround of having voters go through the "Create Ballot" process two or three times to get a single ballot was not going to go over well. No, this all hinged on Cindy getting back with the copies. She should be back by now. Where was she?

Once they had processed the four voters, Carl pulled out his cell phone and entered Cindy's number. There were four rings followed by,

"Hi, this is Cindy. I'm out and about right now so just leave a message and I'll get back to you. Have a great day."

He briefly reflected on how much water had flowed under the bridge since he first heard that message only a few days ago. Three more voters entered the gym.

"Thirty-four," he said softly to himself. "Thirty-four."

48

TUESDAY, 5:55 P.M.

"**I**T'S BEEN AN hour," he said softly to himself. "An hour."
Carl's mathematical equation had gradually altered during the last half hour. Slowly the number of minutes that Cindy had been away was replacing the count of remaining ballots. The two were of course related. Once Cindy returned with the copies, the number of preprinted ballots remaining would become irrelevant. But with each passing moment Carl became increasingly concerned that something might have happened to Cindy.

This concern had not been assuaged five minutes earlier when the radio on the chief's table had come forth with,

"Attention all chief's. Attention all chiefs. We have been carefully monitoring travel conditions and while the interstate is still in good shape many of the side roads are becoming hazardous or even impassable. Therefore chiefs are not to attempt to deliver their election supplies and ballots to the Government Center this evening. I repeat, do not try to drive to the Government Center this evening. Chiefs are to remove their supplies and ballots to a secure place in their homes and return them to the Government Center by noon tomorrow."

Of course Carl knew the "other number" as well. It stood at nine. Nine ballots to go. Wait, make that seven; a couple, apparently husband and wife had just entered the gym.

"Cynthia Pauline Mason"

Carl gave a start. "May I have your ID Cindy—I mean Mrs. Mason?"

Mrs. Mason provided her ID and they went through the check-in process.

"May I ask how the driving is out there?" Carl inquired.

"It's passable for now," Mrs. Mason replied.

Her husband, who was being checked in by Pam, chimed in, "As long as the cars keep using the road during rush hour it should be OK but once rush hour ends it will get nasty."

The Masons were issued their ballot cards and they went back to receive their ballots. Jerry held up seven fingers to Carl.

The Masons marked their ballots quickly and fed them into the scanner. Millicent gave each of them their "I Voted" sticker and motioned them to the side door. As they reached the door, Mr. Mason turned and addressing the room said, "We really must thank you all for doing this. It must be a lot of work."

"You're most welcome," said Millicent with an acknowledging waive. Mr. Mason then turned and opened the door for his wife.

Mrs. Mason let out a startled gasp.

49

TUESDAY, 6:10 P.M.

CINDY STOOD FRAMED in the doorway. At least Carl thought it was Cindy or at least a grotesque imitation of her. As she entered the light of the gym, it became obvious that the past hour had altered her considerably. Her clothes, her shoes, her matted hair were completely soaked. Looking at the left side of her face, it was difficult to distinguish the mud from the bruises; bruises that were punctuated by streaks of recently dried blood. That part of her left wrist that was exposed looked bruised and terribly swollen. In her right hand she clutched tightly her folder.

"Cindy, what in the world?" said Carl.

Mrs. Mason looked at Carl inquiringly but then quickly realized that she was not the Cindy that Carl was addressing.

"Young lady, should I call 911?" asked Mr. Mason.

"No thank you," said Cindy turning to the man. "I took a little spill but I'm fine."

She then turned back and proceeded to Jerry at the ballot table.

"Jerry," she said, trying to speak in a matter-of-fact way. "There should be one hundred copied ballots in this folder plus the one you gave me. I would be obliged if you would count them." She then handed the folder to Jerry.

Having decided that Cindy was among friends, the Masons departed by the side door. At the same time a procession of four new voters entered the gym. They proceeded to the check-in table where they were greeted by no one as the entire team had gathered around Cindy.

"I'm really OK," she repeated. Her voice sounded flat; almost like she was in some sort of trance.

"Of course you are," said Pam. "Why don't you and I take a little trip to the girl's room where we can clean you up a bit."

"No, wait!"

It was Millicent.

"Pam you are needed here," she said pointing to the four voters in the queue. "You are all needed here right now. In addition you demonstrated quite nicely this morning that you can get along splendidly without me. It also so happens that makeovers are my specialty." She held up her rather large handbag.

Stepping forward, Millicent took Cindy's right hand and led her toward the hallway.

"Come with me, my little heroine. We are going to bring you back to the land of the living."

The whole team stood watching Millicent and Cindy disappear through the doorway. Carl then brought them back to attention.

"OK, folks. We still have a precinct to run. Pam, you and I are on the EPBs. Jerry's at the ballot table. And don't forget to count those ballots that Cindy brought. Theodore you're on the scanner. And remember, once we start using the paper copies they go in the auxiliary bin to be counted by hand. I'm not sure how well the scanner would handle them and we don't want to flummox the scanner so close to the end. Now, let's make it happen."

Pam and Carl went back to the EPB table where the voters were waiting to be checked in. The quizzical expressions on their faces suggested that they were not sure if they had just intruded on some sort of intense personal drama.

For the next few minutes they processed a steady stream of voters. By 6:20 Jerry had handed out the last of the preprinted ballots. The next voter, from the check-in table was handed the first of the copies.

"Is this a real ballot?" she asked dubiously.

"Absolutely," reassured Jerry. "It will be counted this evening just like all the others. Now it is paper so please make sure that the ballot is squarely on the table before you mark it."

At that point Millicent reentered the gym and went directly to Carl.

"Here is the key to Cindy's car. Her winter coat and boots are on the front seat. Also in the trunk is a pair of jeans and a sweat-shirt. If you could fetch those, she would be grateful."

"How is she?"

"Shaken up and a bit embarrassed. She's got some nasty welts and bruises that look bad but I suspect they are superficial. A doctor should look at her wrist though. It's badly swollen."

"OK, I'll get her stuff. In the meantime, you take my place here at the EPB table."

"Are you sure? I haven't worked check-in at all today."

"Pam will show you what to do. If you can do first aid, you can check in voters. I'll be back in a flash."

With that Carl hurried from the table and out the side door. The first thing he noticed going down the walkway to the parking lot was that salt had been applied. Apparently that elusive custodian had paid them all a visit.

Carl was able to navigate the ice in the parking lot and reached Cindy's car without difficulty. He quickly found the desired items noting that ice had already begun to form on the windshield. The other cars, including his own, had a more substantial layer of ice. The jeans and sweatshirt from the trunk were filthy but dry. He quickly retraced his steps across the parking lot and entered the gym via the main doorway along with two other voters. He proceeded to the gym and went over to the EPB table.

"Very good, Mr. Mueller," Millicent was saying. "Here is your ballot card. If you will step over to the ballot table you will receive your ballot."

"Here are her things," said Carl, handing the bundle to Millicent.

"Excellent," she said. "I'll get her back here as quickly as I can." Carl couldn't help but notice that since taking charge of Cindy, Millicent had dropped much of her dramatic affectation. He liked the "new" Millicent much better than the old one.

One of the "voters" who entered turned out not to be a voter but a poll watcher, the first they had encountered since midafternoon.

"I'm with the Democrats," he explained, giving Carl his authorization. "I'm here for the closing."

Carl accepted the paper and went back to the chief's table where he quickly found a Democratic poll watcher badge for the man, one Clifton Bowers.

He then returned to the check-in table where he and Pam spent the next several minutes processing the trickle of voters that had been coming in. He had just given a voter her ballot card when Millicent entered the gym with Cindy by her side. She had dried out and changed into her jeans and sweatshirt; most of her facial bruises were covered by what appeared to be a heavy layer of makeup; and her hair was pulled back into a pony tail. She was also favoring her left arm and especially the wrist.

"Our leader has returned," proclaimed Millicent.

"Thank you for everything," said Cindy to Millicent, leaning over and giving her a kiss on the cheek. She then walked over to Carl. Her movements seemed slow and deliberate as if she was testing her ability to fully function.

"I see that the place hasn't gone completely to hell in my absence. Do you have the 6:00 p.m. count?" she asked, trying to keep her tone as businesslike as possible.

"No, we were sort of preoccupied at the time. You see our chief had gone AWOL and we were a bit concerned."

"We'll let it slide this time. What's does the EPB say?"

"Let's see; we are at 614."

"Then we are using the copied ballots?"

"Yes."

They looked at other. Neither one spoke. Neither one had to.

50

Tuesday, 6:30 p.m.

THE STEADY STREAM of voters continued. The same David Brown who had been poll watcher for the Republicans during the setup appeared with his authorization to represent his party during the close.

"You probably should go over the manual to prepare for the close," Carl suggested. Cindy nodded appreciatively. She realized that he was offering her an honorable way of avoiding one of the stations, which given her physical condition was the wise thing to do.

That's an improvement, she thought. *Twelve hours earlier he probably would have said something like "Get out of the way you useless turd so that the rest of us can do some real work."*

And of course there really was quite a bit to consider in doing a successful closing. Cindy knew that Carl could orchestrate it perfectly but tonight that was not his responsibility. It was hers and she wasn't going to hide behind her inexperience or injuries.

She was going over the closing section of the manual for the second time when she became aware that it was only a few minutes shy of 6:45 p.m. This was the time for the "The polls will close in fifteen minutes" announcement which she was required to call out from the front door of the building. She rose and went to the exit, pausing for a moment to get Carl's attention. She pointed at the clock on the wall and he nodded. Cindy then left the gym and went down the hallway to the front door.

From the doorway she gazed over the walkway and surrounding grassy area, illuminated by the flood lamp on top of the school. A steady rain was falling which seemed to be freezing in many places. The ice crystals shimmered as they reflected the light from the lamp.

It really is a pretty sight, she thought, *so long as you don't have to walk or drive in it.*

As Cindy prepared to give her announcement in as majestic a voice as she could muster, a last minute voter came up the walkway. The lone poll worker still working offered him a sample ballot. He was the same young man who had given them the heads-up about the senior bus almost three hours earlier. The voter brushed by him without a word. He approached the door, nodded a pleasant greeting to Cindy, and went past her into the school. Now all that was left was Cindy and the young man.

She left the protection of the awning that hung over the front door and walked slowly down the walkway toward the poll worker.

"You know, if you'd like, you can stand under that awning and get out of the rain," she said pointing toward the door. "You would still be able to see anyone coming up the walkway and get down to here in time to offer them your material before they cross the forty foot line."

The man's coat appeared to be soaked and he was shivering slightly. Still he declined.

"No thank you. It's almost over. I'll stick it out till the end."

"Have you been here all day?"

"I was at Manchester from six to noon; then they had me at Wallingford until 2:45. I've been here since three. They said they would relieve me at five, but so far no one has come."

Cindy was moved by his dedication.

"You must really believe in your candidate."

"Oh yes. Emily Weston really cares about the environment. So many of the politicians don't care. And she has some great ideas and proposals. She can do so much good down in Richmond."

Cindy said nothing. She admired his ideals and agreed with his sentiments but found it hard to share his optimism. She wanted to say something encouraging but suspected it was against the rules and was afraid someone from the "election police" would jump out from the bushes and shout "gotcha!"

"What's your name?" she asked.

"Howard Morgenstein."

"I'm Cindy Phelps. It's a pleasure to know you."

"Likewise, I'm sure," replied Howard.

They shook hands. His hand was cold. So very cold.

"They're lucky to have you, Howard."

"Thank you. It's…it's been a long day."

Cindy glanced down at her cell. The time read 6:45 p.m.

"It certainly has, my friend," she said quietly. "But take heart. In just fifteen minutes, the polls will close."

Howard nodded appreciatively.

Cindy turned and went back to the school, entering through the doorway. She had made her announcement.

51

TUESDAY, 6:55 P.M.

W HEN CINDY REENTERED the gym she returned to the chief's table and began going over, one final time, the procedures for the close; getting the sequence of tasks straight in her mind as well as who she wanted to do each of them. She momentarily forgot that in a few minutes yet another announcement would have to be made.

"Cindy, if you'd like, I can go out and make the 7:00 p.m. closing announcement."

She looked up. It was Carl. She immediately understood. He was allowing her, as much as possible, to stay focused on the upcoming close. The need for her to be on top of things for the close along with the physical soreness she felt, suddenly made Carl's offer seem attractive.

"I'd appreciate it. Thanks," she said.

"Good. I'll be using the number from the Naval Observatory to certify the time. I best get out there now and round up any last minute voters so they can get in here in time." With that, he headed for the exit.

Cindy looked at her cell phone. It said 6:57 p.m. She looked around the room. It was empty save for her team of officers and the two poll watchers. The day was spent. All that remained was to count the votes.

Suddenly a man entered the gym. He was panting and his face was red.

"The man outside said there was still time," he called out to the room at large.

"You're in time," said Pam. "Just calm down and relax and come over here to check in when you are ready."

The man approached the check-in table.

"Gordon Phillip O'Hara," he announced as he handed Pam his ID.

While Mr. O'Hara was being checked in, Cindy went over to Jerry at the ballot table.

"Jerry," she said. "Theodore will be taking down the inside signs but I don't want him battling the elements to get the outdoor ones. Could you gather them up now and bring them in here? I'll give Mr. O'Hara his ballot."

"Sure thing," said Jerry who rose, put on his coat, and exited the gym.

"I'm not finding you in the pollbook, Mr. O'Hara," Pam was saying.

Dear Lord, thought Cindy. *Please let him be in the pollbook. I really don't want to do a provisional at 7:00 p.m.*

"Wait here you are," said Pam. "You're in the pollbook as Ohara without the apostrophe. You may vote."

Wow, what service! I need to pray more often.

"And after you vote, you should fill in a voter registration form with a change of name," Pam continued. She than spoke his name and address out loud and gave him a ballot card.

Mr. O'Hara proceeded to the ballot table and gave Cindy his card in exchange for a ballot. He eyed the paper copy suspiciously.

"Is this a real ballot?" he asked. "It looks like just a piece of paper."

"Yes, it is a real ballot," said Cindy. "It will be counted by hand as soon as the polls close. We ran out of the preprinted ballots a while back and the county authorized us to make these copies. They are real ballots and they will be counted."

"OK," said Mr. O'Hara, apparently satisfied. "Interesting. So when you ran out, you just took a little stroll down the hallway to the copier machine and ran off some new ones."

"Yeah, something like that."

Mr. O'Hara took his ballot over to the table to be marked just as Carl came through the door closing it behind him.

"I made the announcement," he said. "We are officially closed."

Suddenly the radio sounded.

"Attention all precincts. Attention all precincts. The polls should now all be closed. Chiefs are reminded that they need to radio in their results as soon as they are known. Do not wait until all the paperwork is completed. Call in the results first. The political parties are very anxious to have those results. Chiefs should give us four numbers in the following order: number of votes for Haley, number of votes for Weston, number of write-ins, and finally, number of provisional ballots cast."

Cindy went over to the two poll watchers. "We'll be getting started in a few minutes. That final gentleman over there needs to complete his vote and then he will be filling out a form correcting a misspelling in the pollbook. When he exits, we will start the close." The poll watchers nodded.

Just then Jerry came back though the door carrying the outdoor signs which he took to the cart.

For the next few minutes everyone sat in relative silence as Mr. O'Hara marked his ballot, inserted it into the auxiliary bin, and started working on his revised registration. Upon completion, he handed it over to Cindy who reviewed it.

"This looks good," she said. "There won't be any mix-ups or delays next time."

"Well thank you for all you're doing," said Mr. O'Hara. "Have a good evening. I think the rain is beginning to ease up." With that he exited from the building. Cindy looked down at her cell. It was 7:12 p.m.

As she was getting ready to speak, the radio sounded.

"Base, Easthampton is once again first to report. We have as follows: Haley 358; Weston 303; write-ins 1; provisional 0."

The two poll watchers began scribbling notes on their pads.

"Copy that, Easthampton. Thanks for getting the ball rolling."

"OK, gang," Cindy called out. "We have our own ball to get rolling. Pam, you fill out the pollbook count sheet and power down the EPBs. Here's an instruction sheet to walk you through it. When they are finally shut down they go back into the cart."

"Theodore, you take down all the indoor signs and put them back in the canvas bag. Jerry, you close down the scanner. Here is your cheat sheet. When the tape prints there will be three copies; you sign all three. Since we need two sets of signatures on each tape, Millicent you'll be with Jerry. Carl, you and I will hand count the ballots from the auxiliary bin. When anyone finishes their task, see me. If anyone encounters any problems, see me. Any questions?"

There were none.

"Great. Don't worry about doing it fast. Just do it right. OK, let's get started."

52

TUESDAY, 7:15 P.M.

AND SO BEGAN the close.

"Jerry, before you can close the scanner, Carl and I need to retrieve the unscanned ballots from the auxiliary bin. Can we borrow your flashlight?" she said. And then to the poll watchers, "You're welcome to watch us do that if you'd like. You do know that you are required to stay in this room until we radio in the results. At that point you may leave."

Cindy then proceeded to unlock the auxiliary bin and opened its door. Carl then reached in and pulled out the paper ballots. At that point Cindy shined her flashlight into the bin and satisfied herself that it was empty.

"Would you like to look?" she asked the poll watchers. They both took a peek and concurred. The bin was now indeed empty.

"Base, this is Wallingford checking in. We read as follows: Haley 334, Weston 306, write-ins 1, provisional 1."

"Copy that, Wallingford. Great to hear from you."

Mr. Brown, the Republican poll watcher, seemed pleased with the way things were going so far.

Cindy and Carl, however, did not have any time to contemplate the results from other precincts. Carl carried the ballots over to one of the tables.

"How do you wish to proceed?" he asked.

"What I was thinking," Cindy said thoughtfully "is for you to put all the Haley ballots in one pile and Weston's in the other, making sure that none of them stick together. I'll observe. Once that's done each of us will each individually count each of the piles, writing down the totals. We will then compare each of our numbers. If they agree, we're in business; if not we recount."

"That will work," said Carl. "Let me get started."

From the vicinity of the scanner, they could hear Jerry say to Millicent, "OK, we have recorded the protective and public counters on the 7C envelope as these instructions dictate. Next we remove the seal from this little door over here and open it. Ah yes, what does that button say?"

"It says 'Close Poll,'" answered Millicent.

"Right. Now push the button and see what happens."

"Why the screen changes. And on the screen there appears a button that also says 'close polls.'"

"Excellent. Now push that button."

"I did but nothing is happening."

Jerry smiled. "Actually quite a bit is happening. The machine is thinking. In a matter of minutes it will print out the results tape. But for now all we can do is wait."

While this was going on, Carl was slowly dividing the unscanned ballots into the two piles.

"Base, we have our results." It was a voice that Cindy did not recognize. *"We've finished counting the absentee ballots and our totals are Haley 145, Weston 121, write-ins 0, provisional 0."*

"Copy that, absentee. Appreciate the effort."

"So far, you're sweeping the board," the Democratic poll watcher said gloomily to Mr. Brown.

Carl completed forming the two piles. The Haley pile seemed a bit larger.

"OK, I'll start with the Haley pile. You do Weston."

They began their counting. Carl started going through his pile rapidly but Cindy's injured left hand was slowing her down. About halfway through his pile, Carl realized what was happening and he slowed too, but still finished quite a bit sooner. When Cindy was finally done, they switched piles and commenced counting again. This time Carl deliberately matched her pace.

"Base, Seneca Grove checking in. Our totals are as follows: Haley 241, Weston 298, write-ins 0, provisional 0."

"Copy that, Seneca Grove. Nice job."

"Our first win," commented Mr. Bowers. "Now if Manchester breaks heavy for us, we'll be back in business."

"We still have a comfortable lead," countered Mr. Brown.

Cindy and Carl finished their counting.

"I have Haley 25, Weston 18," said Cindy.

"I concur," replied Carl.

Cindy called Theodore, who had completed gathering up the signs, over to their table.

"Take possession of these ballots," she instructed. "Make sure that nothing is added or deleted from the pile. Once the scanner prints its results, these will be put in the blue bin with the scanned ballots but that won't happen for a little while."

Theodore nodded and took possession of the ballots.

Cindy and Carl went over to chief's table where they wrote down the hand counted numbers onto the two identical Statement of Results forms. Those numbers would be added to the scanned numbers when the scanner would finally get around to printing them.

"And now we wait," said Cindy.

"And now we wait," agreed Carl.

"Base, Danby checking in. Our numbers are: Haley 343, Weston 312, write-ins 0, provisional 2."

Mr. Brown pumped his fist into the air.

"Copy that, Danby. Good work today. We're half way home folks. Looking for numbers from Manchester, Hagerman, Chesterbrook, and Cooper."

"We had a late start because of that last 7:00 p.m. voter," remarked Carl. "We could be the last to check in."

Suddenly the scanner started to print its tape even as a familiar booming voice came out of the radio.

"Base, Manchester, the pride and flagship of the district is ready to report its results. We have Haley 488, Weston 686, write-in 3, provisional 1."

"Yes! Yes!" shouted Mr. Bowers.

"Landslide at Manchester," observed Theodore.

"Copy that, Manchester. How are we doing Hagerman, Chesterbrook, and Cooper?"

Meanwhile Cindy and Carl had joined Jerry and Millicent at the scanner. The printer was reporting a lot of numbers that basically confirmed the health of the machine but the counts they were waiting for had not come out yet.

"Base, this is Hagerman," The high pitched voice had also become quite familiar. *"We have Haley 364, Weston 283, write-ins 1, provisional 0."*

"Copy that, Hagerman. Well done. Still waiting on Chesterbrook and Cooper."

By this time both poll watchers were frantically adding numbers trying to see where the election was headed.

"Finally, here it is," shouted Jerry. "It's Haley 316, Weston 284, write-ins 2."

Cindy and Carl immediately returned to the chief's table where they entered the numbers on their respective forms.

"Adding in the hand counted ballots, I have Haley 341, Weston 302," said Cindy.

"Same here," agreed Carl.

She reached over to the provisional ballot envelope and looked inside. "We still have only that one ballot from Mr. Carson. No other provisionals while I was away?"

"None."

"OK, we next need to fill out the call sheet with those numbers," said Cindy. "We'll then use the call sheet to radio in the results. After that we need to tape it on the window of the front door. I guess it's a holdover from the old days before mass communications when people came by in their horse and buggy to see how the election went."

She quickly entered the results onto the call sheet. She then reached for the radio and pushed the button. *"Base, Chesterbrook has its numbers. Haley 341, Weston 302, write-ins 2, provisional 1."*

"Copy that, Chesterbrook. Thanks for hanging in there."

"Pam, could you tape this to the window of the front door? Once she does that our two poll watchers are allowed to leave," said Cindy, handing her the call sheet. Pam took the sheet and a role of tape and headed to the hallway.

"OK," said Cindy, trying to collect her thoughts. "We've given them what they want. Now we still need to do a whole lot of stuff to close this thing out. So next we should—what is it?"

The two poll watchers were looking at each other is disbelief. "Is this what you have?" Mr. Brown asked Mr. Bowers. The Democratic poll watcher nodded. He looked at Cindy.

"Assuming we added correctly the totals are Haley 2,614, Weston 2,611."

"Wow," said Cindy softly. "Separated by just three votes. It looks like Cooper decides it."

53

TUESDAY, 8:00 P.M.

CARL HADN'T INITIALLY picked up on it but one thing had become abundantly clear as the team was working its way through the close.

Cindy was thoroughly in charge.

Looking back Carl realized that she had been at the chief's table studying the manual at various times during the day. In doing so she had obviously mapped out a strategy, relying on the step-by-step process in the manual to be sure, but also leading the team with purpose and clarity. The fact that she was doing this while still in a considerable amount of physical pain made what she was doing that much more impressive.

"Carl," she said, bringing him out of his reverie. "We need to finish the Statement of Results form."

Before them were two forms labeled "Statement of Results" (SOR) and "Statement of Results – Copy." They needed to be filled in identically. Many of the entries included items like the "Number of pre-printed ballots issued," "Number of emergency ballots issued," "final voter check-in number from the EPB," "Number of spoiled ballots," and "Number of votes that were actually cast."

Certain numbers and calculations had to match or explanations for the variance provided. It was rather complex stuff and many chiefs regarded this, coming after being on the go for some fourteen hours, as the low point of a long day.

"I'll fill in the SOR and you'll do the copy," said Cindy. "We will do it side by side in tandem, making sure they are filled in identically."

That made sense to Carl and they began. At various points in the process they needed to extract information from other sources.

"How many spoiled ballots were there?"

"Just the three; all from voters on the senior bus."

"Pam, we need you to count the number of photo copied ballots that were not used."

"Fifty-one," replied Pam after a few moments.

Eventually all the snippets of information they needed were retrieved and they reached the point where the write-in votes had to be entered.

"Jerry, there should be an icon on the scanner screen that allows you to display who got those two write-in votes. Pressing it should do the trick," called Cindy.

"OK, we've got it," said Jerry. "The first write-in vote goes to 'Hank the Cat.'"

"Say, what?"

"That's what it says – 'Hank the Cat.'"

"OK, and the second?"

Jerry paused. "It's really written very small. Can you make it out Millicent?"

"It's more than one line, see that?" said Millicent.

After a few more seconds Jerry read it out loud, very slowly, "Another Republican because I don't like the one they gave us."

"Yes, that's it all right," agreed Millicent.

"OK," said Cindy, turning her attention back to the SOR section on write-ins. "So that's one vote for Hank and one for 'another Republican.'"

"Actually, that's not quite true," corrected Carl. "See it says here that votes for the likes of 'Mickey Mouse' and 'None of the above' are just lumped together as 'Invalid.'"

"So poor Hank doesn't get his moment to shine?"

"It's a short moment. It dies with us."

"So be it," said Cindy as she wrote "Invalid 2" in the SOR.

"I guess that's it," she said, looking at the completed SOR as well as Carl's copy. "Over here everyone. We each need to sign these."

The team gathered around the table and each affixed the required signature. Cindy pulled Jerry aside.

"Jerry, only if you're willing, there's something I'd like you to do."

"Whatever you need," he said. His respect for Cindy's judgment had steadily grown throughout the day.

"Here's the key to my car. Under the front seat is an ice scrapper. If you could clear the ice off people's windshields, it would really help everyone when we finally leave here in forty-five minutes or so."

"I'm on it," said Jerry, who declined Cindy's key. "I have my own scrapper. I'll have that ice removed right away."

Cindy then asked for the tapes from the scanner. The results tape had been printed three times. One copy of each was stapled to the SOR and SOR- copy. The zero report from the opening was also stapled to the SOR.

With the SORs completed, the team was really in the home stretch. Pam removed the blue plastic bin from the large bin under the scanner. This was the bin that contained all the scanned ballots. Theodore then added to that bin the hand counted ballots that he had been zealously guarding. Cindy then closed the flaps of the bin, locked it with her key and had Theodore secure it with a plastic seal. In the meantime Pam powered down the scanner and removed its flash drive which she gave to Cindy. The scanner was then locked and sealed.

It was now a case of making sure that all the large oversized envelopes on the chief's table had the correct contents, were sealed, and had the correct signatures. Cindy orchestrated the proceedings.

"First is the 1A envelope. This has all the provisional ballots plus the log." She looked inside the envelope. "Are you still there Mr. Carson?" She closed the envelope and put a seal over the flap. "Two signatures please." Pam and Carl quickly signed it.

"Next we have the 1B envelope. This is for all provisionals cast after 7:00 p.m. Of course there were none. The envelope is empty." She closed the envelope and put a seal over the flap. "Two signatures please."

"Why are we sealing and signing an empty envelope?" asked Millicent.

"This is not the time to be thinking," said Cindy. "We just do what it says. Sign here please."

"Now we have envelope number 2, the 800 pound gorilla. Let's see. Oath sheet. Compensation sheet. SOR. SOR-copy. EPB count sheet. EPB flash drives, Chief's notes. Paper pollbook." Cindy rattled of the items, ramming them into the envelope. "We'll hold off sealing till the end since the keys go in there as well."

"Next is the 2A envelope. This holds something called the 'Printed Return Sheet.'" She held up a yellow form with spaces for signatures. "Everyone please sign."

"Why are we signing this?" asked Millicent.

"No idea," answered Cindy. "Carl, speak to the woman."

"It's a sheet of paper that says these are the results," said Carl. "See, we are stapling the last of the three results tapes to the form."

"Excellent. Ah, here's Jerry back from the outside. You need to add your signature."

Once everyone had signed the form, it was put in the 2A envelope. Cindy then affixed the seal which was signed yet again with two signatures.

"Now envelope 3, which is not an envelope but rather that plastic blue bin with all the voted ballots. It's already been locked. Now we put on this large seal and everyone signs."

The team gathered around the blue plastic box and signed.

And so it continued. Envelope 4 had the spoiled ballots from the senior bus; there was no envelope 5 (this disturbed Millicent quite a bit); "envelope 6" was a cardboard box where the unvoted ballots were placed; envelope 7C contained the scanner flash dive (Millicent: *Why is there a 7C envelope but no 7A or 7B?*; Everyone else: *Don't worry about it!*); Envelope 8 contained voter registration forms, *Request for Assistance* forms, and poll watcher authorization forms.

And finally it was done. The precinct cart was sealed and locked. All the keys were placed in envelope 2 which was finally sealed and signed. Then all the envelopes along with the radio were rammed into the kit that Cindy would be returning to the Government Center the following day.

Looking around the gym, Cindy took stock. The kit, the blue plastic box, and the brown box of unvoted ballots would go into her car. Everything else would remain behind in the gym to be picked up by whoever.

Cindy tried to think of some words to say to the team. In the end all she could manage was "Well I think we can all say that we have shared an experience today."

And suddenly, spontaneously, they all started to applaud. Pam and Jerry and Theodore and Millicent...and Carl. Each person's face expressed the bond that had been achieved; an expression of their closeness, admittedly just for a single day, that they all felt for one another and especially for the person who had led them.

Cindy was stunned. She was no stranger to praise and applause. But usually it was the result of some well-crafted presentation where people saw her glowing at her radiant best. This was different. Two days ago these people had been complete strangers. They had assembled this morning and for fifteen hours she had led them. They had seen her at her best and at her worst; they had seen her struggle and at times fail. But in spite of her struggles, or perhaps because of them, they had come to appreciate her as a leader and as a person. Cindy was truly touched by their gesture. She tried to find some words to say in response but all she could think of was a simple "Thank you."

54

TUESDAY, 8:45 P.M.

"I'LL HELP CARRY the stuff to your car," said Carl, picking up the brown box with one hand and taking the blue bin by the handle with the other. They left the gym by the side door and proceeded down the walkway to the parking lot. The rain for the most part had ceased but a frosty mist still hung in the air. The cars on the road seemed to be going much slower than usual but at least they were still moving.

They reached their cars. Cindy was glad to see that Jerry had fulfilled his mission. The windshields were all free from ice. At that point they all started to say their individual goodbyes. Pam and Jerry pulled out first, followed by Millicent, and then Theodore. In the meantime Carl considered the best way to get all the election materials into Cindy's car.

The trunk of her car was small and partially filled with things, but Carl managed to rearrange its contents so that the two boxes could fit.

"The kit is going to have to go on the passenger seat, I'm afraid." He then looked dubiously at her left arm and especially the swollen wrist. All during the close she had favored it and Carl thought he had seen her wince in pain at some unguarded moments.

"Are you sure you're OK to drive?" he asked.

"Yes. I'm OK," she said. "I live only a few miles down the road."

"You really should have yourself checked out by a doctor."

"Yeah maybe I will. We'll see."

"Well I guess this is it."

They stood in the parking lot looking at each other. All day long they had struggled with faulty equipment, partisans, the media, political dirty tricks, a shortage of ballots, the weather, and most of all each other but in the end they had accomplished what they had set out to do. Carl just wasn't sure how to end it. Should he shake her hand or give her a hug or what? He sensed from Cindy's puzzled expression that she was wondering the same thing.

He looked into her face. Her eyelids were heavy with lack of sleep. Her hair had come loose from its pony tail and hung limp and matted. Those hideous bruises that Millicent's makeup had camouflaged from a distance were all very obvious now. And Carl couldn't recall seeing anyone quite so beautiful.

Then tentatively, very slowly they both began to inch closer to each other. Cindy began to reach out her trembling hand toward Carl. They were about to touch.

Then her cell phone rang. She pulled back instinctively. The moment was gone.

With a grimace she took out her phone without noting who the call was from. With a harshness that the unknown caller certainly did not deserve she said,

"Yeah, this is Cindy. What do you want?"

"Cindy, this is Roger. I hate to bother you this late, but we have a situation."

55

TUESDAY, 9:00 P.M.

"**N**O, ROGER, No! No more situations. You've used up your quota. We are done. I'm done. We printed the tapes, counted the ballots, and you have the results. Tomorrow I'll bring it all to the Government Center and do whatever you want. I'll dump the contents of the friggin kit onto your friggin desk if it will make you happy. But tonight I am done. I'm going home, pour myself a stiff drink, and watch whatever is on the Horror Channel. It can't be any worse than my last fifteen hours. So you can take your situation and—Carl, what the hell are you doing?"

Carl had just snatched the phone out of Cindy's hand. He put the phone to his ear and turned his back on Cindy.

"Hello Roger. Cindy is a bit indisposed right now. So how's it going out there?—Oh, really—OK, then I better give her back to you."

Then turning back to Cindy,

"Look Roger really needs to speak to you but he needs you to be calm. It's been a long day for him too." Then he added quietly. "I think whatever it is might be serious."

Those few words brought Cindy back to earth. She held out her hand and Carl gave her the phone.

"What is it Roger?"

"It's the Cooper precinct. They have yet to send us their numbers. We've tried contacting them by radio. Nothing. We've tried calling the chief, Julia Hopkins, both on her cell and at her home. There's been no response. It's like they've dropped off the planet."

"Lord Almighty," said Cindy softly.

"We finally got the assistant chief on the phone at her home. She said they wrapped things up over an hour ago but apparently the chief forgot to call in the numbers. The parties are going ballistic. The current count has the two candidates separated by just three votes. Anyway the reason I'm calling is that you are probably the closest person to Cooper who is still in the field."

"Isn't Milton around?"

"Milton isn't available. He had to practically do the whole close at Hagerman. Then Manchester, of all places, called him. It seems they did not have any of the forms required for the closing in their kit so Milton is over there now trying to help them work through it. It appears that the chief never checked the contents of the kit prior to today. Can you imagine that?"

"Unbelievable," said Cindy.

"Cindy, we are hoping that the team at Cooper posted the call sheet with the results onto the front door before they left. The assistant chief couldn't quite remember. Would you be willing to go over to Cooper and see if it was posted and report back to us?"

There was no doubt. There was no hesitation.

"Yes, absolutely. I'll let you know what I find when I get there."

"Thank you, Cindy. We really appreciate it."

Cindy hung up and looked over to Carl. "Cooper never called in. I'm going over there now to see if they posted a call sheet."

"That's five miles away. The roads are a mess and your hand is compromised. You really shouldn't be driving it."

Cindy gave Carl that determined look that he had learned to recognize.

"Don't fight me on this Carl. I know I'm not as invested in all this election stuff as you are but damn it, I swore an oath that said I would see this thing through to the end and for me the end is apparently Cooper Middle School."

Then on a lighter note she added, "There are only three votes separating Haley and Weston so Cooper will decide it. It will be kind of neat to be the first person in the county to know who wins."

Carl was tempted to remark that "anyone who is prepared to drive five miles on icy roads with a busted hand just so she can read some vote totals is a lot more invested in 'this election stuff' than she realizes," but decided it was not the time for such an observation. He contented himself with saying,

"Then at least let me do the bulk of the driving. I lived in New England for three years. I'm a pro at winter driving. Plus I'm not exactly sure your car is built all that well for this weather. You said that your place is just down the road. I can follow you. Drop off your car there and I'll drive us both to Cooper."

Cindy was briefly tempted to compare her sports car with the clunker that Carl was driving but thought better of it. They were on the same side now and his proposal made sense. She nodded a quick "OK" and they got into their respective vehicles.

As Cindy pulled out into the street her thoughts took a more serious turn as she wondered what had happened to Julia, the Cooper chief. She was such a nice old lady and Cindy hoped that she was all right.

56

TUESDAY, 9:15 P.M.

"*W*HILE THE FREEZING *rain has mostly stopped, driving conditions in the county remain extremely hazardous. Traffic on the interstate is flowing without incident but many of the side roads are either treacherous or in some cases impassable. Motorists are advised to use upmost caution or better yet, avoid driving all together.*"

"*On another note, the race for Virginia's 48th State Senate seat between Republican Jennifer Haley and Democrat Emily Weston remains 'too close to call.' With 89% of the precincts reporting, Haley is on top by a mere three votes. This of course, is the contest that will decide which political party will control the Virginia State Senate in the upcoming legislative session. So stay tuned to WADC and we will have the final results as soon as they...*"

Carl turned off the radio.

"There's the school parking lot," said Cindy who had been serving as navigator. "Wow, it's dark. They must have turned off all the lights when the election team left the building."

Carl pulled into the empty parking lot and took one of the spaces closest to the school. They both got out of the car armed with flashlights. Although the precipitation had stopped, the clouds still blocked out any possible moon light.

"This is your turf. Where should we begin?" asked Carl.

"Last November we were in a cafeteria and the call sheet was posted on the main front door, over there," said Cindy, pointing at the door directly in front of them.

"Well then that's where we'll start. But with school in session they would not have used the cafeteria today so that sheet could really be posted almost anywhere."

The two approached the main door, walking slowly on the slippery pavement. They directed their flashlights at the door. As they got closer it became apparent that there was nothing posted on the door or on the other windows immediately adjacent.

"So what happens now?" asked Carl.

"There is no telling what room they used," said Cindy thoughtfully. "Therefore there's no telling what door they would have put the call sheet on. So it's simple; we need to walk around the entire building and check each of the doors. While we're at it we should probably check the windows as well."

"Do you really think that we will find anything?"

"No I don't, but we're here and I want to be able to tell Roger that we did all we could. We can cut our time in half by splitting up. You go clockwise and I'll do counterclockwise. We'll meet somewhere in the rear."

"OK," said Carl, somewhat dubiously. "But walk carefully. It's pitch black."

"No problem. I have balance like a cat."

"Well, the cat's already taken one tumble today."

"Point taken. I'll see you in the back. Oh and when you first spot the beam from my flashlight back there, could you just move your light up and down so I can be sure it's you?"

Too many late nights with the Horror Channel, thought Carl, even as he agreed to Cindy's request. He then turned to his left and started walking past the front of the school. There was a whole series of windows and he shined his light up and down each one. Nothing. He came upon another door but once again there was no call sheet. The cement walkway continued adjacent to the front of the building so the actual walking was easy. As he neared the end of the building, the windows ceased. It was just a solid brick wall.

This must be where the gym is, he thought.

He reached the end of what he assumed to be the gym and made a right turn. Another door; no call sheet. Soon windows began to appear on the side of the building but they were all empty. He continued down the side of the building until he reached the end and made another right turn. He was now in the back of the building. He looked for the beam from Cindy's light but saw only darkness. He started working his way down the back side of the building. There was no pavement here and his progress was slower.

The windows were less numerous here and they continued to be bare of anything that resembled a call sheet. Every minute or so, he gazed into the darkness ahead of him. He wondered what was taking Cindy so long. Gradually he neared the corner of the building. That was when his cell phone rang.

"Carl, I found the call sheet."

This was great news. But something was wrong. Cindy's voice sounded flat. Almost like that wasn't a good thing.

"Where are you?"

"On the side of the building, near the front."

"OK, I'm on my way."

Carl continued in the same direction, no longer hampered by having to check the windows. He rounded the corner of the building and immediately saw the beam from Cindy's light in the distance. Eagerness overcame caution and he broke into a trot.

Approaching Cindy he could see that she was holding something that looked like a wet rag in her hands.

"Where is it?"

Cindy said nothing but reached out and placed the rag in Carl's hand. He looked down at it and saw to his dismay that it wasn't a rag but something that may have at one time been a call sheet.

"Julia taped it to the outside of the window and the tape didn't hold," said Cindy pointing to the large puddle at their feet.

No further explanation was required. The rain had soaked and partially decomposed the call sheet. The ink had ran and the numbers were impossible to read.

"Was this written with a—"

"Fountain pen," said Cindy, completing the sentence. "I remember her using one last November."

Carl studied the sheet trying to decipher anything.

"It looks like the number of write-ins is one," he offered.

"I'm sure Roger will be thrilled with the news. I better call him now."

As Cindy began to place her call, Carl had an idea.

"Roger, this is Cindy. Carl and I are at Cooper. We found the call sheet. Unfortunately it was posted on the outside of an exposed window and the rain ruined it. The paper is soaked and falling apart and the ink has run. We think there was one write-in vote but the Haley and Weston totals are unreadable."

There was a pause as Roger digested the disappointing news.

"OK, Cindy," he said with a sigh. "We knew it was a long shot. I guess we'll just have to wait until Julia shows up with the supplies. Thank you for trying."

"Is there anything else I can do?"

"No you've already gone beyond. Go home and have that stiff drink. Oh, and Cindy..."

"Yeah?"

"You did good today. Real good."

Cindy put her cell phone away.

"So we're done," she said sadly. It was a disappointing way to end the day.

"Not necessarily," said Carl staring at his cell phone.

"What do you mean?"

"I've looked up Julia Hopkins in the Whitepages app. There's a Julia Hopkins, age 88, living on 14 Rosner Place which is—"

"Just a couple of blocks from here," said Cindy, once again completing his sentence.

"We'd be going way beyond—" began Carl.

"I want to do it," she said. "She really is a nice old lady and I'd feel a lot better confirming that she is OK."

"Then let's get going."

They retraced Cindy's steps and returned to the parking lot. The drive to Rosner place was uneventful with overhanging trees shielding the road from the worst of the ice. They arrived at 14 Rosner Place. It was completely dark. Once again, armed with flashlights they got out of the car.

"There's the driveway," said Carl aiming his beam in the appropriate direction. "No car, and let's see…no garage either."

"Look," said Cindy. "There's the morning newspaper on the front walk. It would have come after she left this morning for the 5:00 a.m. opening."

Gradually she began to understand.

"Carl, she never came home after the close."

They stood in silence, staring at the darkened house. Suddenly Cindy gave a start.

"What is it?" asked Carl.

"I think I know where Julia is."

57

Tuesday, 9:55 P.M.

THE CAR SLID down the incline completely out of control. When the skid had started the driver, as the old adage went, "turned in the direction of the skid." Unfortunately he overturned and the car spun completely around so that its front was facing up hill. The driver then tried pumping the breaks in an attempt to get some traction but the car started to slide down the hill. Suddenly the rear end of the car veered off to one side causing it to spin once more. Then at the exact moment that the front of spinning car was pointing downhill, the driver stepped on the gas in an attempt to get it going in the right direction. Miraculously the tires found some traction and the driver recovered a modicum of control. At that point he lightly applied the brakes and the car slowly came to a stop at the bottom of the hill.

Carl and Cindy sat side by side, each in a state of near catatonic shock, both breathing heavily with their faces damp with perspiration. At last Cindy broke the silence.

"I thought you said you could drive on this stuff."

"Snow," Carl replied. "I can drive on snow. This is ice. No one can drive on ice."

"Thanks for the clarification. I feel much better now."

She took a quick drag on her cigarette, her second since they had started their Duncan Hill Road adventure some twenty minutes earlier. "I apologize again for stinking up your car."

"Don't worry about it. However I do think you'd be better off if you quit."

"I did quit, right after college."

"When did you start up again?"

"About eight hours ago."

"Oh—I hope I didn't have anything to do with it."

"Carl, you had everything to do with it. But let's get moving again. We have some miles to go yet."

"Tell me once again why you are so sure she's somewhere on this road."

Cindy explained it again. "When I served at Cooper last November, the chief said that the quickest way to the Government Center was to take Duncan Hill Road to the interstate. Any other way adds quite a few extra miles. Julia had been chief at Cooper for many years. She would have known that."

"But perhaps she made it through."

"If she had then she would have reached the interstate. You heard the radio. It said the interstate was clear. She would have made it to the Government Center long before now."

"What makes you think she even attempted to get to the Government Center tonight? You heard the announcement."

"I don't think it registered. I worked with this woman. She was a delightful companion for the first half of the day but by early afternoon she began to lose it. She was completely zoned out after 3:00 p.m. I think muscle memory or something took over. And you saw her house; she never came home."

Carl wasn't completely convinced but there was no choice but to continue. Retracing the miles of winding icy roads that they had just traveled was not an option.

"So let's see," said Carl studying the rise directly in front of him. "It starts as bare pavement, then it gets ice, and who knows what is at the top. So I guess we just step on it and hope for the best."

The car lurched forward and built up some initial speed before coming into contact with the ice. Its momentum carried them past the initial patch but eventually the tires started to spin. Carl turned the wheel to the right and the car began to move forward again. He then quickly turned the wheel back to the left and the wheels found some dry pavement. In a moment they were at the top of the hill where a stretch of relatively dry roadway awaited them.

"Can I open my eyes?" asked Cindy who had been staring down at her lap.

"For the moment."

Having reached the top, Carl now allowed the car to continue in its forward direction. He was however taking no chances, never letting the speedometer exceed twenty, even though the pavement looked bare.

He remained silent for a few minutes, working up the nerve to say something that he had been wanting to say for a while. Finally he spoke.

"When this is done, one way or another, we're proceeding to the interstate."

"Oh?"

"Two exits from here is the hospital. You are going to the ER."

"Like hell I am. I feel fine; my wrist is fine."

"Your wrist is swollen up like a balloon. And if you feel fine, I suspect it's because you swallowed a whole bunch of pain killers when you took your election things inside your apartment."

Cindy sat in sullen silence for a few moments.

"I only took two."

"I'm not a doctor but I suspect you could do some real damage if it's not treated. They'll probably put it in a cast or a heavy bandage or something."

Cindy was not convinced. "And I'm not about to be taken to the hospital by someone I've known for scarcely a day, who I don't especially like, and who has been making my life miserable for the past twenty-four hours."

"Look over there. Where the road starts to bend," said Carl who had ceased to follow what she was saying.

"I see it," said Cindy excitedly. "The car is definitely off the road. I can't tell if the front is in the bushes or hit a tree or—"

Cindy sighed, "False alarm. It's just parked at the end of the driveway."

They took the turn slowly and started down a dip in the road. Fortunately the traction remained good.

"I lied," said Cindy.

"Excuse me."

"I lied just now."

"No you didn't. The car was in the driveway."

"Not about that. What I said before."

"Oh?"

"When I said I didn't like you."

They came upon an icy patch and Carl began to pump the brakes lightly. They reached the bottom of the dip and started up another rise.

"Well, aren't you going to say something? Like maybe you like me, perhaps a little?" asked Cindy.

Carl considered. "I'm not sure I should be the one telling you this…"

"Yes?"

"But you're not the easiest person to like."

The car was silent for a few moments. Then,

"That's what my boyfriend said."

"Your boyfriend?"

"Well my ex-boyfriend actually. We had four wonderful months together. Then he told me what you just told me and left. I guess it took him four months to figure out what you gleaned in only twenty-four hours."

"Cindy."

"Yes?"

"It didn't take me twenty-four hours."

"Well I'm certainly glad we cleared that up," said Cindy, putting out her cigarette.

"Actually we haven't cleared up anything. I said 'you're not the easiest person to like.' I did not say—"

"Oh my God! Do you see that?"

"I see it. And I need to be going very carefully because—see that ice we're approaching."

There was indeed a nasty stretch of ice near the bottom of the hill that they were descending. And then at the very bottom of that hill the road took a sharp right turn and off to the left, sticking out into the road, was the tail end of a car.

Carl took his foot off the gas and pumped the brakes lightly, hoping to keep his car under control. They slowly passed the disabled vehicle and then Carl successfully navigated the right turn. At that point he pulled into a nearby driveway and turned off the engine.

Cindy was out of the car in a flash running to the disabled car as fast as she could.

"The front of the car is into a tree," she called back to Carl. "And there's someone in the driver's seat."

That was all Carl needed. He whipped out his cell phone and dialed 911.

"Emergency line."

"I'm reporting a car that went into a tree. There's a person in the front driver's seat. We are located on Duncan Hill Road about six miles from the turn off Carter Road."

"Honey, Duncan Hill Road has been closed for the last hour. The Department of Transportation notified the police to barricade all the entrances."

"Well there was no barricade when we entered about twenty minutes ago."

"Carl, it's Julia," Cindy shouted. "She conscious but shaken up. I can't really tell if she is injured or not."

"Now that's interesting," said the operator. "Communications between DOT and the police is not all that good sometimes. You see they are down at the end of the hall and it's a long hall—"

"Yes ma'am. We really need an ambulance. And they may have a tough time getting here. There's a lot of ice."

"Don't worry. They can get through anything. I'll get them started right away."

With that Carl was out of the car racing to Cindy and the disabled vehicle. She was talking to Julia, holding her hand.

"I've called 911," said Carl. "They're on their way."

"I'm sorry to put you to all this trouble, young man," said Julia. "I sort of lost control back there. I think I bumped my head."

"You're doing fine," said Cindy. "Just keep talking to me."

"Why I think I remember you," Julia said to Cindy. "We did one of the elections a while back. I have today's election materials in the back seat somewhere."

"Don't worry about that now. You're doing fine."

For the next fifteen minutes Cindy and Carl took turns talking to Julia. At last the sirens of the ambulance could be heard. Carl ran out into the road to flag them down. After a minute he saw the bright headlights and started waving his arms. The ambulance came to a halt.

"It's over there," he said pointing to Julia's car. The paramedics got out and quickly took control of the situation.

Having done all he could do, he then took out his cell and dialed the Government Center.

"Roger. We found Julia Hopkins. She was apparently trying to drive out to the Government Center when her car hit a tree. There isn't any obvious injury but the paramedics are with her now."

"We told everyone not to attempt it tonight. Apparently she missed the message."

Then after a pause, Roger continued.

"Carl I hate to even mention it but are the election materials in Julia's car? The political parties are apoplectic with rage right now. Biff Logan is threatening to sue the entire county. The parties need to have those numbers."

Carl had always prided himself in his devotion to the electoral process. Yet twice that very day events had occurred to remind him that there were times that this process, as important as it was, must yield to other imperatives. The first had come earlier when he had refused to support Cindy's removal. Now standing in that icy road, watching the paramedics hovering over Julia, he responded to Roger's request in the only way that seemed to make any sense.

"Roger, tell the parties to go to hell. A chief who the county should have never appointed just drove her car into a tree while another chief that you all wanted to fire a couple of hours ago has risked life and limb to track her down. In the fullness of time you will get your results. In the meantime why don't you all have a stiff drink and chill out? I understand there's something good on the Horror Channel. I'll call you back when I have something to say but it might not be for a while."

And with that Carl hung up.

Looking up he saw the paramedics wheeling Julia on a stretcher toward the ambulance.

"How is she?" he asked one of them.

"I think she's OK," was the reply. "But with her age you don't want to take any chances. We'll bring her in to the ER for a look over."

"Do you know where the young lady who was with her is?"

"Can't say that I do."

Carl looked around. Then he saw a beam from of a flashlight coming from the back of Julia's car. He went over to the car and peered inside.

Cindy was in the back seat hunched over what appeared to be Julia's kit. Wedged between her swollen left hand and the back seat was the Cooper Statement of Results form. In Cindy's right hand was the radio.

"Base, this is Chesterbrook calling. I've been authorized by the Cooper chief to give you their results. I repeat, these are the numbers for Cooper. For Haley..."

58

JANUARY 11

Electoral Board confirms Senate contest
By J. C. Styles, Washington Herald

In a rare Sunday session the county Electoral Board has confirmed the results of last Tuesday's special election where Republican Jennifer Haley apparently defeated Democrat Emily Weston by a mere 11 votes or less than 0.2% of the 5,884 votes cast. The final confirmed tally remains as it was called unofficially Tuesday night: Haley 2,943, Weston 2,932, with 9 votes going for various write-ins. As a result of this election, the Republican Party will continue to hold a majority of seats in the State Senate, a position they have held since the resignation of Lieutenant Governor-elect Wilbur Norris.

Election officials were quick to discount any controversy concerning the delayed reporting of the results by one of the precincts Tuesday night. It was described by Electoral Board president Kate McGowan as a "communications misunderstanding that was quickly resolved by election personal." McGowan also emphasized that all necessary paperwork from each precinct was delivered to the Government Center by noon, the day following the election as *prescribed by the election code and all materials were secured in the appropriate way.*

The Electoral Board has also reiterated their earlier condemnation of the actions of a group calling itself "Virginians against Fraud."

"The contents of their heavily edited and misleading video completely misrepresents what went on at the Chesterbrook precinct. There was never any danger of anyone voting fraudulently and the board stands 100% behind the actions of the chief election officer in her handling of the incident," declared board president McGowan.

It is not known whether defeated candidate Weston will be requesting a recount as allowed by law. "The closeness of the race almost dictates it," said Democratic Party County Chair Brian "Biff" Logan. He admitted however that "the canvass conducted in the days after the election uncovered no irregularities and pointed to perfect execution on the part of all election personnel."

Epilogue

LATE MAY

"**H**ELLO, THIS IS Cindy Phelps. May I help you?"

"Hey Cindy, it's Deb. How's it going?"

"Hey Deb. You know, same old, same old. What's up?"

"Two things. A whole bunch of us are going to see the Nationals play in June. We'll be ordering tickets in the next couple of days."

"Sounds great. Who are they playing?"

"Who cares? We're meeting at the beer garden right outside the park at 5:30. Should we write you in?"

"Absolutely. What day is it?"

"Tuesday, June 9."

"Oh no. I'm afraid I have a conflict that day."

"What? Family stuff? Or do you have a hot date?"

"No, nothing like that. The political parties are having their primary elections that day and I've signed up to be chief election officer."

"Are you kidding? The last time you did that you wound up in the ER—"

"Yeah, but it wasn't that bad."

"—with a concussion—"

"That was never fully verified."

"—and a broken wrist—"

"Actually it was just a bad sprain."

"—that had you in a sling for a month."

"You're making it sound really bad."

"And just how do you make it sound good? Good grief girl, you even started smoking again."

"Just for a couple of weeks. I've quit for good, now."

"So you say. Can't you get out of it? Tell them your company is sending you out of town or something."

"I could, I suppose…but I really want to do this thing."

A pause.

"I worry about you Phelps. Are you becoming some sort of election nerd?"

(laughing) "God, I hope not."

"Are you sure? Something's up. Like that night we were at Houlihan's. And we ran into those guys and you started talking about John Quincy Adams. That was so weird."

"It wasn't just John Quincy Adams. You see it was John Adams, John Quincy Adams, Martin Van—"

"Stop, you're freakin' me out. Anyway, I get the message. No Nats game. The other thing is that next Thursday is Mary's birthday and we're taking her to the Cheesecake Factory. Are you good for that?"

"You bet. Count me in."

"Are you sure? No one is electing an alderman that day or anything?"

"No, not that day. I'm good."

"OK, talk to you soon. And let me know if you change your mind about the Nats game."

They exchanged a few final pleasantries and hung up.

An election nerd, Cindy wondered. *Is that what I'm becoming?*

Well I guess there are worse things to be, she thought as she leaned back in her chair and gazed fondly at the framed photo on the corner of her desk.

GLOSSARY

The terms included in this glossary are used in the narrative of the book and are explained when they initially appear in the text. They are included here to aid the reader in following the story and are not intended to represent the specifics of any real life voting locality.

Election Officers are one day volunteers who serve on Election Day. They receive a small stipend for their service and are required to take an oath that they will conduct the election "according to law and the best of their ability."

Chief Election Officer is the election officer who is ultimately responsible for the running of the precinct. He/she directs and assigns the other officers and handles all the non-routine situations. In Virginia, the chief election officer is generally of the same party as the sitting governor.

Assistant Chief Election Officer is "second in command." He/she must be of the opposite political party from the chief. If the chief becomes unable to perform his duties, the assistant chief takes over.

Rovers are seasonal employees, generally former chiefs, who on Election Day drive a preassigned "route" of precincts. They provide the chiefs on an "as needed" basis with extra supplies, technical assistance, advice, and/or encouragement.

Poll watchers are representatives of the political parties who are authorized by the parties to be inside the polling place on Election

Day. They are required to present their authorization to the chief upon entering the polls. They may observe but not hinder the activities inside the polling place.

Poll workers are partisans who hand out literature for the candidates. They require no authorization and must conduct their activities at least forty feet from the entrance to the polling place.

Pollbook is the listing of the registered voters in a precinct. Until recently most precincts used **paper pollbooks** which consisted of binders that contained a line entry for each voter. Voters were "checked in" using the paper pollbook.

In recent years many localities have gone to **electronic polls books (EPBs)** which are computer laptops that contain the same data that used to be in the paper pollbooks. Looking up voters in the EPBs is a lot faster than with the paper pollbooks but most localities still issue the chief a paper pollbook as backup in case there are technical problems with the EPBs.

Privacy folder is a plain manila folder. Individual ballots are placed in the folder before being given to the voter. This allows the voter to maximize his sense of privacy.

Privacy Booth – three sided cardboard structures which are placed on tables. The voter sits down at the table and works on his ballot which rests within the perimeter of the booth, thereby maximizing his privacy.

Provisional ballots are cast is situations when a voter cannot be confirmed as being a registered voter in the precinct. A provisional ballot is placed in a special envelope and is not scanned or in any way counted on Election Day. Generally a phone call is made to the Government Center to attempt to resolve a voter's situation before a provisional ballot is issued. Three days after the election, the Electoral Board meets and determines whether each of the provisional ballots will be counted.

"The cart" is a metallic crate on wheels that contains the electronic poll books, boxes of ballots, privacy booths, privacy folders, handicapped ballot marking machines, signs, posters, extension cords, and additional supplies. It is delivered to the precinct, locked and sealed, from the county warehouse several days before an election.

Canvas bag – contains many of the generic signs, posters, and forms that are used in every election. The canvas bag is generally stored in the cart.

"The kit" is a suitcase on wheels that is issued to the chief at the pre-election meeting. It contains many of the forms and signs that are specific to the current election (as opposed to the more generic signs that are in the canvas bag) along with other supplies.

Scanner is the voting machine of choice in many localities. The ballot is fed into the scanner which records its vote internally, even as the ballot drops into a bin under the scanner. At the end of the day a tape prints out the result.

"Create Ballot" (fictitious brand name) is a touch screen ballot creation device that allows a voter to mark his/her selections by touching the desired candidate's name on the screen. This machine is primarily for handicapped voters who might experience difficulty in marking a preprinted ballot. The session is initiated by an election officer inserting a blank card into the machine. After the choices are confirmed the machine returns the card with the selections made. That card is then inserted into the scanner which recognizes it as a completed ballot.

Zero tape is printed by the scanner at the start of the day. It confirms that no votes have been cast and that each candidate has zero votes.

Results tape is printed at the end of the day with the number of votes for each candidate. Generally, three copies of the results tape are printed which are affixed to different documents.

Auxiliary Bin is a bin where ballots are placed that for some reason cannot be scanned at the time they are cast. At the end of the day they are scanned (if possible) or otherwise counted by hand.

Statement of Results form is the official document of the election. It contains the final results of the election as well as other relevant counts such as the number of ballots issued to the precinct, the number of unused ballots at the end of the day, the number of ballots spoiled, number of provisional ballots cast, etc.

Call sheet is a form where the results of the election are written down. The numbers from the call sheet are called into the Government Center on election night and those numbers are released to the press as the unofficial results. The sheet is then posted on the door of the polling place for the general public to see.

About the Author

BILL LEWERS WAS raised on Long Island in the 1950s and has been a political junkie for as long as he can remember. He holds B.A. degrees from Rutgers (mathematics) and the University of Maryland (history) and a M.A.T. degree from Harvard (mathematics education). After teaching high school mathematics for a few years, he commenced a career as a computer professional with IBM, retiring in 1999. He lives in McLean, Virginia with his wife Mary.

Bill is a lifelong fan of the Boston Red Sox and this passion is reflected in his first book, *Six Decades of Baseball: A Personal Narrative.* This was followed by *A Voter's Journey* which is one citizen's sixty year romp through the American political system. *The Gatekeepers of Democracy* is his first venture into the world of fiction.

77407869R00167